The Marquis paused before he said very quietly, "I love you, I love you with my heart and my soul. How soon, my Darling, will you marry me?"

Imilda moved to hide her face against his shoulder.

"I have . . . something to . . . tell . . . you," she said in a voice he could hardly hear.

"What is it?" the Marquis asked.

"I am . . . not who you . . . think I . . . am," Imilda whispered. "I am . . . in . . . hiding."

"In hiding?" the Marquis questioned. "From whom?"

After what seemed a long silence, Imilda whispered, "From . . . you."

A Camfield Novel of Love
by Barbara Cartland

"Barbara Cartland's novels are all distinguished by their intelligence, good sense, and good nature. . . ."
— **ROMANTIC TIMES**

"Who could give better advice on how to keep your romance going strong than the world's most famous romance novelist, Barbara Cartland?"
— **THE STAR**

Camfield Place,
Hatfield
Hertfordshire,
England

Dearest Reader,

Camfield Novels of Love mark a very exciting era of my books with Jove. They have already published nearly two hundred of my titles since they became my first publisher in America, and now all my original paperback romances in the future will be published exclusively by them.

As you already know, Camfield Place in Hertfordshire is my home, which originally existed in 1275, but was rebuilt in 1867 by the grandfather of Beatrix Potter.

It was here in this lovely house, with the best view in the county, that she wrote *The Tale of Peter Rabbit*. Mr. McGregor's garden is exactly as she described it. The door in the wall that the fat little rabbit could not squeeze underneath and the goldfish pool where the white cat sat twitching its tail are still there.

I had Camfield Place blessed when I came here in 1950 and was so happy with my husband until he died, and now with my children and grandchildren, that I know the atmosphere is filled with love and we have all been very lucky.

It is easy here to write of love and I know you will enjoy the Camfield Novels of Love. Their plots are definitely exciting and the covers very romantic. They come to you, like all my books, with love.

Bless you,

CAMFIELD NOVELS OF LOVE
by Barbara Cartland

A NEW CAMFIELD NOVEL OF LOVE BY

Barbara Cartland

Passage to Love

JOVE BOOKS, NEW YORK

PASSAGE TO LOVE

A Jove Book / published by arrangement with
the author

PRINTING HISTORY
Jove edition / November 1995

ISBN: 0-515-11751-X

A JOVE BOOK®
Jove Books are published by The Berkley Publishing Group,
200 Madison Avenue, New York, New York 10016.
JOVE and the "J" design are trademarks
belonging to Jove Publications, Inc.

PRINTED IN THE UNITED STATES OF AMERICA

10 9 8 7 6 5 4 3 2 1

Author's Note

THE terrible conditions I have described in this country in 1817 after the war had ended are exactly what occurred at the time.

Sir Arthur Bryant, in his brilliant book *The Age of Elegance*, tells us of the suffering of the farmers when cheap food from the Continent came into the country.

He also writes of the unspeakable frustration of men who came back from the war without pensions and without jobs waiting for them.

A great number of people died of starvation and undoubtedly a number took "to the road" merely to steal enough money to keep themselves alive.

It is true that the Duke of Buccleuch and Lord Bridgewater did what they could on their Estates.

But there were plenty of harsh Landlords who rack-rented their land to finance their extravagances and many more who, absorbed in their pleasures, refused to be troubled.

But eventually, as always happens in our history, the English were roused to try to improve the situation and, as always, eventually got back to normality.

All wars leave misery and destruction behind them, and the Napoleonic Wars had lasted far too long.

As Dryden wrote:

> " 'Tis well an old age is out
> And time to begin a new."

chapter one

1818

"DID you enjoy the Ball last night?" the Countess of Harsbourne enquired.

Lady Imilda looked up and replied:

"Yes, it was quite amusing, Stepmama, but much the same as all the Balls I have been to this week."

"Did you get a proposal of marriage?" the Countess asked.

Lady Imilda looked at her in surprise.

"A proposal!" she exclaimed. "I only danced with one young man whom I had met before and, quite frankly, I found him dull."

The Countess frowned.

"I think you are being rather tiresome, Imilda," she said sharply. "After all, let us be frank and say that the sooner you are married, the better."

Lady Imilda's eyes opened wide in astonishment.

"I cannot think why you should say that," she said. "I have no intention of getting married unless I am in love. I do not want to spend the rest of my life with a man with whom I have no interests in common."

The Countess made a sound of irritation and then said:

"I have been meaning to speak to you for some time, Imilda. I do not think you understand that you are very fortunate to be a *débutante* with a rich Father who is also important."

She paused and went on positively:

"You are having two Balls given for you, and in consequence everyone in the Social World invites you to their parties. But that is something that will not continue for ever."

"I cannot think why not," Lady Imilda objected, "and to rush into marriage is surely a mistake."

She was thinking, as she spoke, of two girls who had been her friends at school, although they were older than she was.

Both of them had married when they were *débutantes* and had been very unhappy in their marriages.

Imilda had made up her mind long before she came home from her Young Ladies Academy and Finishing School that she would have to be very much in love before she married.

It never occurred to her that her Stepmother would have other ideas.

Now she said a little tentatively:

"Surely you and Papa do not want to get rid of me so quickly?"

"It is not a question of getting rid of you," the Countess said, "but my duty as your Stepmother is to see that you make an important marriage as soon as possible after you are eighteen, which you are now."

"I am sure my Mother, if she were alive, would not think like that," Lady Imilda said quietly.

"I am quite certain she would," the Countess contradicted her flatly. "I have talked it over with your Father, who agrees with me that girls should marry when they are young if they are to make a good marriage with the approval of their families."

"But suppose I want to marry someone of whom you do not approve?" Lady Imilda asked provocatively.

"That question shall not arise," the Countess snapped, "and if it does, your Father will deal with it."

Lady Imilda sighed.

She had never cared much for her Stepmother, and had been desperately unhappy when her Mother died.

They were two very different people, and she now realised even more the difference between them.

Her Mother had been someone who always found the best in everyone, so that for her the world was an enchanting place, almost like the fairy-tales which she had read to Imilda.

She had followed these with the stories of the Knights of the Round Table and the poetry of the Troubadours.

After that came the plays of Shakespeare, all of which Imilda found entrancing.

She could hardly believe it when only a year after her Mother died her Father married again.

Her Stepmother was a very beautiful woman, but as Imilda's old Nanny had said at the time, "Beauty is only skin deep."

The new Countess was practical, energetic, and enjoyed organising other people's lives.

She had managed to make her Husband undertake

a great number of activities he had never contemplated before.

This had undoubtedly increased his importance in the Political and Social World.

Imilda now thought with horror that her Stepmother intended to manage her too.

She was quite certain that if she was not careful, she would find herself being led down the aisle by some young Peer she hardly knew.

That he had a title and a large Estate would be all that mattered.

She had learned, however, from experience that it was a mistake to fight with her Stepmother if it could be avoided.

Now she said in a much more conciliatory tone:

"I am sure, Stepmama, you are doing what you think is best for me. But I do beg you to understand that I want to find the man of my dreams, the Prince Charming I have read about in books, before I marry."

The Countess pressed her lips together.

She made her face, beautiful as it was, somewhat hard and unpleasant.

"I was talking to some of the Dowagers last night," she said, "and they all agreed that you looked the most attractive and the prettiest girl in the Ballroom. Surely one or two of the men with whom you were dancing told you so."

"They paid me compliments," Imilda admitted.

"What about Lord Cecil, whose Father is a Duke? What did he say to you?"

"He talked only about his horses, and obviously has no interest in anything else."

The Countess frowned.

"And what about Lord Renishan? He is certainly a

very good-looking young man."

"I think from what I can remember of his conversation," Imilda replied, "he was mostly concerned as to which pack of hounds he would hunt with next Winter. In fact, now I recall he asked me a great number of questions about the Hunt to which Papa belongs."

"Well, all I can say," the Countess admonished, "is that you cannot be trying to attract a young man the way that you should. I had three proposals in my first Season, all of them from men of distinguished families, and I was not as fortunate as you are to have an Earl for my Father."

Imilda knew quite well the pleasure it had given her Stepmother to have an Earl for a Husband.

She had been married before to a rather dull Baronet who was very much older than she was.

When he died of a heart attack, she was still young and beautiful enough to attract men.

There was no doubt that she had picked out the Earl of Harsbourne as the most important man available.

She had made herself seemingly indispensable to him.

Imilda could understand her Father had felt lonely and rather helpless without his wife.

He had been glad to find a woman who apparently not only loved him but admired everything he did.

She had also flattered him into making him believe he could play a more important part in his world.

It would be unfair to deny she had been successful in proving this.

It was only, Imilda thought, that she had no wish to have her Stepmother interfering in her life also.

She was not concerned as to whether a young man

she was dancing with was blue-blooded and was to inherit a title.

As her Mother had, she liked people for themselves.

If she was honest, she had so far been disappointed in the men she had met at dances.

Granted, they were all very young.

The older unmarried men avoided *débutantes* and their ambitious Mothers like the plague.

They spent their time either with attractive married women or with the alluring Cyprians who were the toast of St. James's.

Imilda thought secretly that it would be very difficult to compete with them.

She could understand that men found them far more interesting than shy and rather gauche *débutantes*.

They had hardly been allowed to meet any men until they left the Schoolroom.

As it happened, Lady Imilda was extremely intelligent.

Her Mother had said so often:

"You ought, Darling, to have been a boy. It would certainly have pleased Papa to have a second son."

Imilda's brother, the Viscount Bourne, was at the moment abroad.

When they were growing up as children together, she had shared his Tutor with him.

When he went to Eton and on to Oxford, she had deliberately kept up with his studies at both places.

She had insisted on discussing the subjects in which he was interested, in the holidays.

Her brother William often said to her:

"You are far cleverer than I am, Imilda. We ought to exchange places, you the boy and I the girl."

They had laughed at the idea.

Imilda had, however, enjoyed being proficient in Latin and Greek as well as French.

She had a greater knowledge of the Classics than William.

She had been very disappointed when she was presented at Court and became a *débutante* that William was not there.

He had been very apologetic because he loved his sister, but as he said to her:

"I shall never get a chance like this again, so how can I refuse?"

The chance was, in fact, a visit to India with the son of a new Governor and the possibility of a great deal of wild-game shooting.

Of course Imilda could understand why he wanted to go.

Now she wished desperately that William were there.

He would be able to think of the right arguments with which to persuade her Stepmother that she was not to marry precipitately.

The Countess could read her thought and said:

"I know you are thinking of William and looking forward to his return to England. But you must be aware that sooner or later William will marry, and his wife will certainly not want you hanging around him as you always do, and sharing with him everything he does."

"I love being with William, Stepmama," Imilda said. "I find it such fun to discuss things with him and argue over subjects of which hardly any young men and no girls know anything."

"Well, I think it is a lot of nonsense," the Countess said. "Let me make it quite clear that no sensible man wants a wife who is cleverer than he is and keeps telling him so."

She hesitated for a moment before she said:

"Tonight we will be at another Ball, at which I hope you will be more successful than you have been at the others."

She paused a moment before she continued:

"Then on Friday we are going to the country for the Steeplechase which your Father organises every year. I have not yet had a list of the men taking part, but I will go and look it over and see if I can persuade your Father to include at least one young man who might offer you his heart."

Then she went from the room, leaving Imilda alone.

Imilda jumped up and walked to the window.

She looked out at the small garden which lay behind the house her Father owned in Park Street.

She wished she were in the country.

At least then she could do what she always did when she had a problem—go riding.

There were horses in the Mews on which she and her Stepmother rode in Rotten Row.

But it was not the sort of riding she enjoyed when she was at Harsbourne House in Hertfordshire.

There she could gallop over her Father's Estate.

She could jump the hedges and the fences he had erected.

"What am I to do?" she asked herself. "It is an absurd idea of Stepmama's that I must get married immediately."

It had never struck her that for a *débutante* that was considered the crowning glory of her Season in London.

Now she looked back over the plans that had been made for her.

She could see how determinedly her Stepmother was using her organising powers to get her to the Altar.

"I shall have to fight this every inch of the way," Imilda told herself.

She wished again that William was with her.

That evening her Father joined them before they went upstairs to dress for dinner.

The Earl said to his wife:

"We shall have eight men staying in the house for the Steeplechase; the rest will be with our neighbours."

"I have been meaning to ask you whom you have invited," the Countess replied.

The Earl reeled off seven names, and then he said:

"And lastly this morning I persuaded the Marquis of Melverley to join us."

"Melverley?" the Countess exclaimed. "I had no idea you knew him."

"I knew his Father well," the Earl replied. "Melverley Hall is not much more than twenty miles away from us in the country. But since the young Marquis inherited the title, he has, I understand, never gone back to Melverley, which has naturally upset the people on his Estate."

"Why has he not gone home?" Imilda enquired.

"I do not rightly know," her Father replied, "except that he is certainly making a reputation for himself in the *Beau Monde*."

"In what way?" Imilda asked.

The Earl looked towards his wife as if he thought it would be a mistake to answer his daughter directly.

"If you want the truth," the Countess said, "the Marquis is behaving abominably."

"He won a medal for gallantry when he was with

Wellington," the Earl interposed.

"He may have done that," the Countess said, "but ever since his return from the Army of Occupation he has spent his time upsetting a large number of distinguished men who have no wish to have their wives compromised and talked about."

"You mean," Imilda said, wishing to get it clear, "that he has had a number of love affairs?"

"Far too many," the Countess snapped. "One day, you mark my words, he will get into real trouble!"

"It seems a pity," the Earl said, "because he is a nice young man and, I am told, very intelligent."

"Who is the latest in the long list of ladies whom he has favoured with his attentions?" the Countess asked in a sarcastic voice.

"I believe it is that Italian beauty," the Earl replied, "the *Contessa* Di Torrio. I have seen her once or twice, very beautiful, and I should suspect as fiery as a cannon ball."

The Earl laughed at his own joke, but the Countess glanced at Imilda and the Earl said quickly:

"Well, whatever else he may be, he is an outstanding horseman and I shall be surprised if he does not win the Steeplechase."

"That completes our House Party," the Countess said. "Counting Imilda, we will have eight women staying to balance your riders, besides, of course, the Referee and his wife and your friends the Duke and Duchess of Crowcombe."

There was undoubtedly a little lilt in the Countess's voice when she mentioned the latter.

It always gave her a thrill to entertain people with distinguished titles.

This was the first time since she had married the Earl that the Duke and Duchess of Crowcombe, who were old friends of his, had stayed at Harsbourne House.

The Countess was in a good temper for the rest of the evening.

When they drove home later from the Ball, she did not, to Imilda's relief, ask her questions about her partners.

Instead, she talked of leaving the next day for the country.

She was finding the arrangements which had to be made for the Steeplechase rather complicated, especially with many of the competitors staying in the house.

"I expect," the Countess said, "that after travelling and with the Steeplechase the next morning, everyone will be ready for an early bed. As you know, this party is really for older men, and you will, in fact, be the only young, unmarried girl."

The Earl's Steeplechase took place every year.

The Countess was quite right in saying that the men were rather older but not too old to ride with.

The ladies who came to applaud them were either widowed or married to complacent Husbands who had other interests of their own.

They were not interested in riding in a rather difficult Steeplechase.

The Steeplechase had not taken place last year owing to the death of the Earl's wife.

The year before, Imilda had been too young to go downstairs to dinner.

Instead, she had peeped at the party from the Minstrels Gallery in the Dining-Room.

She had been very impressed with the beauty of the ladies as they sat round the dinner-table.

They certainly looked magnificent.

They had tiaras on their heads, which, of course, only married women could wear, and diamonds round their necks and in their ears.

The laughter which filled the Dining-Room was a relaxed, but at the same time, an exciting sound.

Imilda had felt it was a scene in a fairy-tale in which one day she would take part.

Yet now that she was actually in it, she had to admit to herself that she found it somewhat disappointing.

The beautiful women were there at the Balls, and the handsome, well-dressed men who accompanied them.

But no-one gave a Ball or a party which was exclusively for *débutantes*.

They were just tucked in, so to speak, at those given for their elders and betters.

If they received little attention, they were granted no right to grumble.

They were expected to be grateful that they could at least look on at those who really enjoyed the excitement.

If William had been riding in the Steeplechase, Imilda knew she would have enjoyed it enormously.

As it was, she would be watching a number of men she did not know and was not at all concerned who lost or won.

She was aware only that her Stepmother was in a tizzy of excitement about the whole thing.

She was determined that the party should be a success.

To her it was all-important that the members of the House Party should enjoy themselves and say so when they returned to London.

"Are you not going to ride, Papa?" Imilda asked her Father.

She remembered he had won the race when she was twelve.

"I am going to be one of the Judges," the Earl replied. "I am getting too old to risk my neck and exhaust myself on such a ride."

"Oh, Papa, how disappointing!" Imilda cried. "I would like you to be the winner."

"I think that will be young Melverley," the Earl answered, "he is only twenty-seven and already has proved himself in a number of different ways which are entirely to his credit."

"And a great number entirely to his discredit," the Countess rejoined.

"I think you are being rather harsh on him," the Earl said. "Wellington would not have rewarded him for gallantry if he had not earned it. And, of course, it was sad that his Father died when he was in the Army of Occupation."

He paused for a moment before he said:

"Now that I think of it, I suppose Melverley is one of the richest men in Britain besides having inherited one of the oldest titles. The Melverleys as Earls go back to William the Conqueror."

The Countess did not say anything, but Imilda knew she was impressed.

She was unlikely now to be so critical about the Marquis's behaviour.

They set off for Harsbourne early the next morning.

The Earl drove his travelling-Phaeton, which was built for speed, and took with him the Countess and Imilda.

There was no room for anyone else except the Groom, who was perched up behind.

The luggage, the Lady's-Maids, the Earl's Valet,

and a number of the other servants followed in a large brake.

There was always a large staff at Harsbourne House.

However, on special occasions like the Steeplechase, footmen and extra hands in the Kitchen came down from London.

It always caused somewhat of a commotion, but to Imilda it was interesting to see how once they arrived back home, everything sorted itself out.

They drove down the drive with its avenue of Lime trees.

She saw her home in the distance looking very impressive in the early afternoon sunshine.

It had been in the family for three hundred years.

The Earl's Father had added to it a Picture Gallery which meant having a whole new wing built onto the existing house.

The gardens were glowing with spring flowers and to Imilda it was all very beautiful.

"If only William were here," she murmured as she ran to the Stables immediately after they arrived.

The horses, which she hated to leave during termtime, were there.

There were also visiting horses, a number of which had already been sent by their owners to take part in the Steeplechase.

There were some new additions to the Stables which her Father had told her about when he wrote to her at School.

She shook hands with the Chief Groom, and the Stable-lads were pleased to see her.

"We've got some spirited horses for ye to ride, M'Lady," they told her, "and ye'll find 'em difficult to handle."

They all knew what a good horsewoman she was.

When she said she must return to the house, the Chief Groom said:

" 'Tis a pity, M'Lady, that with the Viscount not here ye can't take his place in th' race."

"I wish I could," Imilda said, "but you know they would be shocked if I did, and absolutely furious if I won."

He laughed at this.

"That be true enough, no man ever likes being beaten by a woman."

"Who are you putting your money on?" Imilda asked.

She knew that the Stable-men always had a bet on the Steeplechase and any other race her Father arranged.

"Oi fancy th' Marquis o' Melverley," the Chief Groom answered. " 'E be a fine rider for all 'e's been neglecting 'is home an' never putting a foot inside it. 'Tis not right, as th' whole neighbourhood has been saying for a long time."

Imilda thought he must be a very irresponsible young man to neglect his own people.

She knew her Father took a personal interest in everyone on his Estate.

If anyone was ill, her Mother always insisted on being told about it and did what she could to help.

"If he behaves like that, I hope he does not win the Steeplechase," she told herself.

They had arrived at Harsbourne House in time for a late luncheon.

The afternoon was spent with the Countess fussing over the arrangements of the rooms which Imilda thought was quite unnecessary.

The Steeplechase had been held for many years and

most of the servants had been with them since she was born.

They knew exactly which Bedrooms to use.

Although Imilda was not aware of it, the House-keeper was well aware who should be next door to whom, or just across the passage.

The Countess was, however, making changes, and that, Imilda thought, was a mistake.

However, it did not concern her, and she went to her own Bedroom, where she had slept since she left the Nursery.

It was exactly the same as it had always been.

The same maid who had always looked after her was unpacking her box.

"Here I am, Betsy," Imilda said. "It is lovely to see you."

"Ye be a sight for sore eyes, M'Lady," Betsy said. " 'Tis time ye came home here instead of tiring yeself out with all those festivities in London."

"You are quite right, Betsy. It is lovely to be home and to find such good horses in the Stables."

"There be plenty o' 'em," Betsy said, "and we'll be talking of horses all tomorrow and until the party leaves."

Imilda laughed because she knew this was true.

She then started to change her clothes.

Her Stepmother told her she was to be downstairs in plenty of time before dinner to greet the new ar-rivals.

"As most of them are coming a long distance," she said, "they had better go up to their rooms as soon as they arrive. Then there will be Champagne in the Drawing-Room, before dinner."

Imilda made no reply, and the Countess went on:

"Tonight there will just be the guests staying in the

house, but tomorrow, when our neighbours come to dinner after the Steeplechase, your Father will arrange for there to be gambling and Bridge afterwards."

Imilda had heard all this before, so she did not really listen.

She was wearing one of the pretty gowns which had been bought for her as a *débutante*.

It was, of course, white, but trimmed, as was the fashion, round the hem and *décolleté* with small roses glittering with *diamanté*.

"Ye look real lovely, M'Lady," Betsy said, "and that's th' truth. I've never seen a gown like that afore."

"It is the fashion and very expensive," Imilda said. "I expect most of the other guests, if they are married women, will be blazing in jewels."

"And paintin' their faces!" Betsy added.

Imilda knew that married women added powder, rouge, and a little salve to their lips in London.

They were, as a rule, somewhat more discreet in the country.

Imilda knew that country-women like Betsy were shocked.

She herself thought, however, that they looked rather pretty, though perhaps a little theatrical.

"At least I do not have to trouble to do it," she told herself, "until I am married."

Because her skin was white and almost translucent, it seldom needed powder.

Her perfectly shaped lips were pink without any addition to them.

Her hair was fair, or, rather, golden, with just an unexpected touch of red in the candle-light.

Imilda knew that she resembled her Mother.

A portrait of her by Sir Joshua Reynolds made her

very beautiful and at the same time spiritual.

It was almost as if she were not of this world but had stepped down from Olympus.

"That is how I want to look," Imilda told herself when she looked at the portrait.

When she went down to dinner she was thinking of her Mother rather than the people she would meet.

There were already two or three men in the Drawing-Room when she entered it, and her Father introduced her.

Two of them were old friends of his whom she had met before.

They told her how much she had grown and was now as pretty as her Mother.

"That is what I wanted you to say," Imilda said as she smiled, "but I know I will never really be as pretty as Mama."

More people were coming downstairs, including the Countess.

She was in a fluster because she was later than she intended to be.

"Forgive me," she said. "I had so much to see to. I do want you to enjoy this party and it to be a success."

"We always enjoy it," one of the men said. "It is something I look forward to every year."

"I hope you have a really good horse for tomorrow," the Earl said. "My Stables are full with the best collection I have ever seen."

They all started to talk about horses, until the Butler announced from the door:

"The Most Noble Marquis of Melverley, My Lord."

The Earl hurried forward to greet him.

"Forgive me for being late," Imilda heard the Marquis say. "I went straight upstairs to dress so that I would not do anything so appalling as to keep dinner waiting.''

He was laughing as he spoke, and the Earl said:

''That would indeed have been an unforgivable sin. Let me introduce you to my wife and daughter.''

The Countess was beside him, and he looked round, as he spoke, for Imilda.

She walked forward to join them.

''I am so delighted you could come and stay, My Lord,'' the Countess was saying, ''and I am told by everyone here that you are likely to be the winner of the Steeplechase.''

''I shall be extremely humiliated if I am not,'' the Marquis answered.

Imilda thought it was rather a conceited remark.

Then her Father was saying:

''This is my daughter, Imilda, who has come out this Season.''

The Marquis held out his hand.

As she looked at him, Imilda realised he was extremely handsome, and at the same time well aware of his own consequence.

Their hands touched.

Then, as if she were of no importance, the Marquis turned to her Father.

''You must tell me, My Lord,'' he said, ''who are my rivals. I am determined to win the cup which I understand you always give to the winner of the Steeplechase.''

''I have given nine,'' the Earl said, ''and this will be the tenth.''

''I hope that is my lucky number,'' the Marquis replied.

A servant offered him a glass of Champagne and he lifted it up.

"To the Harsbourne Steeplechase Cup," he said, "and may it be mine."

"That is certainly a toast which has not been given here before," the Earl said as he smiled, "and I suppose I can only wish you the best of luck."

"Why should you do anything else?" the Marquis enquired.

They went into dinner, and Imilda found herself sitting between two men who had ridden in the Steeplechase several times before.

They were reminiscing over the past.

They talked ostensibly to Imilda, but at the same time they could not help talking over her head to each other.

They exchanged some rather unkind and malicious jokes about their contemporaries.

Then one of them said:

"I suppose Melverley will be our stumbling block tomorrow."

"Is he really as good as he thinks he is?" the other man asked. "I have never seen him ride."

"Nor have I," was the reply. "But if he is as good with horses as he is with women, then we have something of an obstacle in front of us."

"If he spends his time in London," the other said contemptuously, "going from Boudoir to Boudoir, I can hardly believe he is as fit as he should be."

"Now, Crawford, over there," he added, nodding towards the other side of the table. "has been practising for weeks at his place in the country, so as to be really fit tomorrow, and have a real chance of snatching the cup from us."

"I wish I could say the same," the first man complained. "Unfortunately I had to speak in the House of Lords last night, and I was on an important committee the night before. There was no chance of my getting away."

"Me neither," his Companion replied. "Nevertheless, we will do our best and no man can do more."

Imilda said nothing.

She was watching the Marquis of Melverley, who was obviously causing trouble.

He was flirting with a very pretty woman sitting next to him.

She had arrived with a rich and rather important Baronet, who was sitting on the other side of her.

Imilda could see that he was getting annoyed because she was neglecting him and giving the Marquis so much attention.

There was no doubt she found what the Marquis was saying to her not only amusing but also pleasingly complimentary.

Imilda could not hear what he was saying.

But the Beauty fluttered her eyelashes at him, pouted her lips provocatively, and occasionally gave him a very encouraging smile.

'I suppose that is the way the Marquis always behaves,' Imilda thought, 'and that is why he has such a bad reputation.'

She was wiser than she knew.

By the end of dinner the Baronet's eyes were dark with anger and his lips pressed into a tight line.

Watching him, Imilda thought it was a fascinating situation to watch.

There was no doubt a drama was developing, a drama in which the Marquis, while he was behaving like the villain, would undoubtedly walk away with the heroine.

Her Stepmother took the ladies out of the Dining-Room, leaving the men to their port.

Imilda found herself in the Drawing-Room near the lady who had been sitting next to the Marquis.

She was talking to another woman, who was obviously a friend.

"Oh, my dear, he is fascinating, absolutely fascinating! I can quite understand why Ruby wanted to commit suicide when he left her."

"And Cecilia," the other woman said, "cried her eyes out for a month and no-one could do anything with her. If you ask me, he casts a magic spell over them."

"Yes, it really is something like that," the first speaker said. "He has a charm that other men do not have, and you feel he is almost compelling you to listen to him. Poor old George was furious, but I will make it up to him."

"Do be careful, Vera," the other woman said. "If you fall in love with Melverley, you know it is only a question of time before he is bored and you are left disconsolate."

Vera laughed.

"But think how amusing it must be," she said in a soft voice, "before he is bored."

chapter two

It was a relief to find the next day that the sun was shining and there was no chance of it raining.

Imilda got up early and went to the Stables.

She wanted to look at the horses before they were taken round to the front of the house.

The Stable-hands were all discussing amongst themselves who they thought would be the winner.

There was no doubt the favourite was the Marquis.

When Imilda went back for breakfast, she found all the men were downstairs.

The ladies were having breakfast in their Bedrooms.

"We have plenty of time," the Earl said, "we do not start until eleven o'clock, and it is a good idea to look at the course first, and make quite sure you do not make any mistakes."

"I remember there was rather a tricky place last time I rode in the Steeplechase," one of the guests said, "and at least two men went wrong."

"I do not think that will happen again," the Earl

said. "The course is marked very clearly."

There was nothing else to talk about except the Steeplechase and the horses.

Imilda listened with considerable interest.

The ladies arrived down soon after half-past ten, looking very glamorous.

They had, as Betsy said, painted their faces and wore very pretty gowns.

They were exceedingly encouraging and complimentary to the men in whom each one was interested.

Imilda noticed that quite a number of them wished the Marquis "good luck" in soft, rather sensuous voices.

'It is not surprising,' she thought, 'that he is so conceited, since they never leave him alone.'

The number of competitors was larger than the Earl had expected.

Additional riders had come with some of his neighbours.

He had to tell the Countess there would be more people for luncheon than had been planned.

Once they started, everyone was tense with excitement.

The course was laid out at a place on the Earl's Estate where more than half of the race could be seen by the spectators.

Some years ago he had erected a Stand which accommodated a large number.

The seats were made comfortable with cushions, and there were rugs in case anyone felt cold.

"There is one man well out in front, I wonder who it is?"

"I am sure it is the Marquis," another woman said.

"I am not so sure," was the reply.

There was, however, no doubt who it was when they came nearer.

The Marquis was three lengths ahead of the rest of the field.

There was one man who made a desperate effort to overtake him in the final straight.

But the Marquis, by sheer good riding, won by a length fairly comfortably.

There were cheers from members of the House Party.

Only those who had backed a local rider grumbled, and Imilda heard one woman say:

"He should be handicapped."

The Marquis received many congratulations, and those who had backed him cheered loudly when later he accepted the silver cup from the Earl.

After that they went up to the house for luncheon.

There were about forty places laid in the large Dining-Room.

The Earl made a speech congratulating those who had taken part, and was followed by the Marquis.

Imilda could not help acknowledging that he spoke well and managed to be quite amusing at his own expense.

After that they had an unexpected speech from one of their neighbours.

He said he wished to thank the Earl for the pleasure he had given everyone.

He then congratulated the riders for being even finer horsemen than they had been in previous years.

It all took a long time.

When everyone had left, it was time for tea.

When that meal was finished, most of the ladies went upstairs to rest before dinner.

Imilda felt she was unwanted and went to her own

room with a book she wanted to read.

Her room was on the same corridor as her Father's State Bedroom.

She found, to her surprise, that the Marquis had been given a room on that corridor also.

It had always been kept for the family because Imilda's Mother had wanted her children with her.

As soon as they were old enough, she took them out of the Nursery and put them in the State Rooms next to her own.

"I want this corridor to be kept for the family and the family alone," she insisted.

Imilda remembered that her Father had been rather surprised.

"Those rooms, in my parents' days," he said, "were always kept for Royalty or very important guests."

"No-one in the house is more important than my children," his wife had answered, "except, of course, yourself, Darling."

The Earl had smiled.

"Very well," he said. "We will not bother to entertain Royalty if we can help it."

"You are all the Royalty I want in my life," his wife said softly.

Imilda now saw the Marquis walking into the room next to William's and opposite her own.

She supposed that her Stepmother was being snobbish in giving him one of the most important Bedrooms in the whole house.

Tonight there would be thirty for dinner.

A few of their neighbours were to come in afterwards to dance or, if they preferred, to play cards.

As they were going upstairs, Imilda heard several of the women saying they would prefer to dance.

"Harry lost far more money than he could afford last night," one woman said. "I can only be grateful that we went to bed early."

"I love dancing," the other woman replied, "and Peter is a very good dancer. But I also like a game of Chance, especially when someone else pays up if I lose!"

Several women laughed at this.

But Imilda thought it very strange, although she knew it often happened.

How could women who were covered in jewels let a man who was not their Husband pay their losses?

She was, however not particularly interested and opened her book, which was a history of the Tudors.

When she came down to dinner, she found to her surprise that she was sitting next to the Marquis.

She had supposed he would be on her Stepmother's left with the Duke on her right.

Then she saw that the Lord Lieutenant had come to dinner, and he, of course, was next to the Countess.

As dinner started, she realised the Marquis was flirting in an animated manner with the lady on his other side.

She was another staying in the house.

Imilda could not help thinking with amusement that the man to whom she was supposed to be attached would be feeling like a Baronet last night!

He would be grinding his teeth with jealousy!

On her left she had one of her Father's old friends.

He was having an argument with the lady on his other side about the new rules which had recently been announced by the Jockey Club.

Imilda was not at all worried that neither of them wanted to talk to her.

She looked round the table, watching the other people.

Unexpectedly a man in the party who had already had a great deal to drink, said:

"I think we should have started this meal by drinking the health of the winner today. It may be a bit delayed, but I am going to toast the best rider I have seen for years—The Marquis of Melverley."

He lifted his glass as he spoke.

Because it was only polite to follow suit, everyone lifted theirs.

"To Melverley!" a man shouted. "He's a jolly good fellow!"

He sang the first few words of the song, and then, as no-one joined in, hastily drained his glass.

Everyone else drank a little, but Imilda put her glass down untouched.

She thought the Marquis had had quite enough praise and this was really overdoing it.

As ordinary conversations started to buzz again, to Imilda's surprise the Marquis turned towards her.

"I noticed, Lady Imilda," he said, "you did not drink my health. Was that for any particular reason, or have you had enough Champagne already?"

Imilda paused for a moment, and then she replied:

"If you want the truth, I thought there was too much fuss about something that is not of real importance."

The Marquis looked surprised.

"Not of real importance?" he repeated. "That seems a strange thing to say about your Father's Steeplechase."

"They were drinking to you and not the race," Imilda replied.

"So you do not think that I am important enough?" the Marquis asked.

Imilda had the feeling that while he was astonished at being criticised, he was genuinely interested to know the reason.

"I suppose," Imilda said, "that is the truth. I feel as far as you are concerned, My Lord, there are so many much more important things which should command your attention."

"What in particular?" the Marquis asked in a slightly hostile voice.

"If you really want to know the answer to that, I will give it to you," Imilda replied. "But it may be something you do not want to hear."

"Of course I want to hear it," the Marquis said sharply.

"Very well," Imilda said. "If you want the truth, I find it extraordinary that a man of your importance is not at this moment fighting to put this country back on its feet after the ravages of war."

The Marquis stared at her as if he could hardly believe what he heard. Then he said:

"As perhaps you know, I fought on the Peninsula and at Waterloo so that we could have peace. Is that not enough?"

"Not really," Imilda said, "for someone in your rank and with your influence. What matters now is to see that having won the war we win the peace, and in that we are failing dismally."

The Marquis stared at her again. Then he said:

"What exactly do you mean by that?"

"Surely it is not difficult for you to understand," Imilda said, "that the majority of the men who have come back from the Army of Occupation have found, as did those who returned when the war ended, that there are no jobs and no pension from a grateful Government."

The Marquis hesitated for a moment, and then he said:

"I am sure, if they look, they can find work. I always understood, for instance, that the farmers were short-handed."

"That was during the war," Imilda answered. "Since the war ended, cheap food has been pouring into England from the Continent, and the farmers are having a very tough time. In fact, a number of them are finding it difficult to make a living at all."

The Marquis did not speak, and she realised he had not been aware of this.

"You must have learnt, if you read the papers," she went on, "that many of the Country Banks have failed and with that the farmers lost their savings."

The Marquis was silent.

"As I was saying, there are therefore no jobs on the land, and unless a man steals or lives on the goodwill of his neighbours, he starves."

"I had no idea," the Marquis murmured, "that things are as bad as that."

"Well, they are," Imilda said, "and I think that someone like you should be bringing it to the notice of those responsible for the running of the country."

"But surely they must be aware of what you have just said to me," the Marquis suggested.

"What is essential in order to get anything done about it is to arouse public opinion," Imilda said, "and you, My Lord, have a platform in the House of Lords."

"That is true," the Marquis said, "although I doubt if anyone would be interested in what I have to say."

"I cannot believe you are quite as modest as that," Imilda replied. "You are a hero from the war, and although there were others, not one of them has spoken for the wounded men who came back to England after Waterloo. They were left crippled and starving without a pension and without anyone to put their case before Parliament."

There was a little sob in her voice, and the Marquis said:

"I was, as you know, serving in France after the war ended. Surely someone cared for these men?"

"Only the people in the villages from where they had come. Those who had no relatives or friends were forced to beg or steal every crumb they swallowed."

"I swear to you, I had no idea of this. Of course something should have been done for them."

"That is what many people have said, but nothing was done about it," Imilda rejoined.

"And now?" the Marquis asked.

"Things are slightly better, but, as I have said, the farmers are not only finding it difficult to sell their crops, but there is no-one to speak on behalf of their troubles and their difficulties and make it a National Problem."

The Marquis was silent, and Imilda knew he was genuinely thinking over what she had said.

She did not speak for a minute or so. Then she said:

"What is needed in war is leadership, and the same is no less needed in peace."

The Marquis seemed about to reply to her, when the lady with whom he had been flirting attracted his attention.

"You are neglecting me," Imilda heard her say in a plaintive little voice.

Before the Marquis could respond, the Countess

rose at the end of the table to lead the ladies from the Dining-Room.

As she went, Imilda wondered if she had said too much.

Somehow the words had come out without her really weighing what she should say.

She just knew it was a waste of a man who had so much to give his Country, but was, in her opinion giving so little.

There was a small but excellent Band playing in the Ballroom.

When the Gentlemen joined the Ladies, the Countess led at least half the party along the corridor.

The strains of a violin could be heard invitingly in the distance.

Imilda did not lack partners.

The Marquis did not come into the Ballroom, but stayed with some of the men who were gambling.

Finally, at midnight the Earl said that as it was Sunday, the music must stop.

He added that in his opinion everyone should go to bed.

There was laughter at this.

The men who had been riding confessed they were feeling tired.

But the women would have gone on dancing and gambling if their host had not more or less driven them upstairs.

The Ladies went first and Imilda went with them.

When she went into her Bedroom she thought with a sigh of relief that the weekend would soon be over.

She wanted to ride with her Father.

She much preferred to be alone with him, just as in the old days she had ridden alone with William.

'I suppose,' she thought to herself, 'Stepmama will

be annoyed with me for not having flirted with any of the men who were here tonight.'

But with the exception of the Marquis, they were all, in her eyes, more or less nonentities.

It was not, she thought, that they were not pleasant, it was just that they did not have much personality.

Nor were any of them doing anything of importance in the the world.

'Perhaps I am asking too much,' she thought as she undressed. 'But the Country has to face so many problems at the moment that no man should spend all his time just enjoying himself.'

She had heard the men laughing and comparing notes about the amusements they found in London.

The women, when they had come from the Dining-Room, were talking in low voices.

It made Imilda sure they were confiding in each other about their various love affairs.

She had told Betsy not to wait up for her.

The woman was tired after what had been a long and busy day's work.

She hung up her gown in the wardrobe and put on a pretty nightgown.

She blew out the candles on the dressing-table.

Then she thought that the room seemed rather hot.

She pulled back the curtains, and as she did so, thought she heard the door of her room open.

But, as she fixed the casement so that it would not blow about in the wind, she decided she must have been mistaken.

She pulled the curtains together so that she would not be woken too early with the dawn.

Then, as she turned round, she saw in the light of the candles by her bed something on the floor at the far side of the room.

For a moment she could not think what it was.

Then its eyes flashed in the light and she was suddenly aware it was a rat.

It was a very large rat facing her.

If there was one thing that Imilda really loathed, it was rats.

Because it was so unexpected and it frightened her, she screamed.

It was not a very loud scream, but the rat stiffened.

She suddenly felt terrified it might rush at her and bite her.

She screamed again and called out:

"Help! Help!"

The door of her room opened and a man asked:

"What is the matter?"

"It is . . . a rat! A . . . huge . . . rat!" Imilda cried.

As she spoke, the rat had run under the bed and disappeared behind the chintz flounce.

The man at the door came further into the room, and Imilda saw it was the Marquis.

"A rat?" he asked. "Are you quite sure?"

"Quite . . . sure . . . and he has . . . run under . . . the bed."

The Marquis stared at the bed as if he did not know what to do about it.

Then a voice from the doorway asked sharply:

"What is going on here?"

It was the Countess.

She came into the room and exclaimed:

"My Lord! Why are you in Imilda's Bedroom?"

"I heard a scream," the Marquis explained, "and your stepdaughter tells me there is a rat in the room."

"A rat!" the Countess exclaimed scornfully. "I have never heard such nonsense! There are no rats, or mice for that matter, in this house, I can assure you."

"That is ... not ... true," Imilda asserted. "A rat ... has just ... run under ... the bed."

"A likely story, and not at all original!" the Countess retorted. "I think, My Lord, you should go to your own Bedroom, and my Husband will speak to you in the morning."

The Marquis looked at his hostess.

Then, as he understood exactly what she was implying, his lips tightened.

Without saying a word he walked away.

The Countess and Imilda were alone.

"There *is* a rat ... here," Imilda insisted.

"I just do not believe you," the Countess said. "I think His Lordship's behaviour is disgraceful, and I can assure you that your Father will think so too."

She went out of the room, closing the door behind her.

Imilda gasped.

Then she realised with horror that she had been left alone with the rat.

She picked up a candle by the bed, and, opening the door, went into the passage.

There was no-one about because the rest of the guests were sleeping on other corridors.

Imilda merely crossed her corridor and went into William's room.

It was as familiar to her as her own.

William had his own special treasures hung on the walls and a bookcase filled with his favourite volumes.

The bed was not made up, but Imilda did not worry about that.

She just slipped in between the blankets and put her head down on a pillow which did not have a linen cover.

For a moment she felt so bewildered by what had

occurred that she could not think clearly.

Then, as her heart started beating less frantically, she realised that it was a trap.

It had been set by her Stepmother and had succeeded in catching for her exactly what she wanted.

Imilda knew that the presence of a man in a young girl's bedroom would, if known, ruin her reputation.

The only honourable course for a man under the circumstances was to offer her the protection of his name in marriage.

Lying on her back in the darkness, Imilda told herself her Stepmother had thought it all out extremely cleverly.

Tomorrow her Father would speak to the Marquis.

It would be impossible for him as a Gentleman not to accept the responsibility and offer to marry her.

It sounded so fantastic, she could hardly believe it herself.

Now she remembered that when she opened the casement she had thought she heard her door opening.

That had been the moment when the rat had been put inside her room.

She had wondered why the Marquis had been put in one of the rooms which were never used except on very special occasions.

Now she knew with horror that her Stepmother was organising her life as she organised everything else.

It would be very difficult, if not impossible, for the Marquis to find a way out of the trap she had set for him.

In the turmoil of her mind Imilda found it impossible to sleep.

She tossed from side to side until finally the dawn broke.

She hoped then that perhaps what had happened

last night was just a figment of her imagination or a bad dream.

Yet she knew she had not slept at all.

By the time the sun had risen, she was determined to prove to herself, and if possible to her Father, that there really had been a rat in her Bedroom.

She was very frightened of rats.

It was, therefore, with the greatest difficulty that she forced herself to cross the corridor.

Then, as she reached her Bedroom, she found the door was open.

She was quite certain she had shut it when she had gone to William's room.

In fact, she could remember quite clearly doing so, almost as if even then she wished to keep the rat inside.

Now she knew that after she was safely in bed, her Stepmother must have opened the door to let the rat escape.

It would certainly not remain in the room with which it was not familiar.

There were no holes in the wainscoting into which it would vanish.

Imilda was sure she need no longer be afraid it was still there.

At the same time, she moved cautiously across the room to draw back the curtain over the window.

The rising sun came streaming in.

The room looked as beautiful and cosily familiar as it had ever since she had first slept in it.

Imilda forced herself to look under the bed and beneath the wardrobe.

There was, of course, nothing there, nothing, she thought, to prove that her story was genuine and that a rat really had frightened her.

It was then that she got into her own bed.

She tried to think of what she should do.

How could she save the Marquis from having to acquiese in what, if her Stepmother had her way, would be demanded of him.

It all seemed an insoluble puzzle.

Having been awake all night, Imilda at last fell asleep.

She did not wake until, to her astonishment, it was half-past ten.

Hastily she rang her bell, and a few minutes later Betsy was with her.

"So ye're awake, M'Lady," she said as she came into the room. "Her Ladyship said I were to leave ye sleeping. I've never known ye be as late as this. I'll get yer breakfast."

Before Imilda could say anything, Betsy hurried away.

When she returned, she said:

"There's no hurry, M'Lady. His Lordship has gone to Church an' them in the party who're still here be sitting in the garden."

"Who is left?" Imilda asked.

"Two of th' Gentlemen who were riding and th' Ladies they comes with have gone back to London," Betsy said. "And th' winner of th' race, th' Marquis, he went very early. His Lordship had a talk with him before he were dressed."

Imilda gave a sigh.

She had wanted to talk to the Marquis before he saw her Father, but now it was too late.

Betsy was tidying up the room, and after a moment Imilda asked:

"Do we have many rats in the house, Betsy?"

" 'Tis funny ye ask that, M'Lady," Betsy replied. "I haven't seen a rat for ever so long. Then yesterday morn' Mr. Duncan caught a real whopper down in th' cellar.''

"A big rat," Imilda murmured.

"Very big, an' ye'll not believe it, but he happened to tell Her Ladyship what he'd caught an' she asked him to keep it alive for her. Now, wasn't that funny? I've never known anyone want a rat afore.''

Imilda did not answer.

She knew now exactly how the idea had come into her Stepmother's mind.

The rat had provided her at exactly the right moment with what she wanted.

Betsy went on talking about the party, but Imilda was not listening.

She was wondering what she should do when her Father spoke to her about the Marquis as she was certain he would do.

Because she was tense and upset, the party seemed to drag on indefinitely all day Sunday.

It was not until Monday morning that all the guests had returned to where they had come from.

"It has been a wonderful party," most of them told the Countess, "and we have enjoyed every minute of it.''

The Duke and Duchess said the same thing, and the Countess was delighted.

"It is so nice, my Dear," the Duchess said, "to find that Harsbourne House is just as comfortable and charming as it has always been.''

The Countess was all smiles.

The Duke and Duchess drove away in their comfortable carriage drawn by four well-matched horses.

"It has been a great success, my Dear," the Earl said to his wife.

"As long as you are pleased, Darling, that is all that matters," she replied.

"I am certainly pleased about the arrangements you made," the Earl answered, "and now, Imilda, I want to speak to you. Come into the Study."

This was the moment Imilda had anticipated.

She followed her Father across the hall and down the passage to the Study.

As she went, she was wondering frantically how she could persuade him that the whole thing was just a ridiculous joke on the part of her Stepmother.

When they entered the Study, her Father crossed the room to stand with his back to the fireplace.

"I have very good news for you, my Dearest," he said. "Very good news indeed."

"What is it, Papa?" Imilda asked in a very small voice.

"When he left unexpectedly early this morning." the Earl said, "the Marquis of Melverley asked my permission to pay his addresses to you."

There was a little pause before Imilda said:

"Did he . . . ask you . . . without . . . any preliminary explanation . . . as to why he should do so?"

The Earl looked embarrassed.

"You must understand, my Dear, that your Stepmother was very perturbed at finding the Marquis in your Bedroom last night."

"Did she explain why he was there?" Imilda asked.

"I should have thought that was obvious," the Earl replied. "It is not what I expect of a Gentleman."

"The Marquis came to my room because I screamed for help," Imilda said. "There was a huge rat in my room, and I very stupidly have an aversion to rats."

"That is what your Stepmother told me you had said when she discovered you and the Marquis together," he answered.

He was looking very stern when he went on:

"You cannot expect us to believe such an extraordinary tale, and even if it were true, the Marquis, with his reputation, had no right to be in the Bedroom of a young girl who has only just come out."

"Listen, Papa," Imilda pleaded. "It was a trap set by Stepmama because she wants me to marry someone grand. I have no wish whatever to marry the Marquis, just as he has no wish to marry me. I absolutely refuse to marry him."

"I am sorry you should feel like this," the Earl replied, "but you must realise, my Dearest, that your whole reputation is at stake. Your Stepmother says that she saw several men coming up the stairs who had not yet turned towards their own rooms, and they may have seen the Marquis going into yours. You know as well as I do what gossip is like as far as he is concerned."

"I will not marry him, Papa, whatever you say."

There was a silence and then the Earl said:

"The Marquis told me much the same story as you have told me, but whatever his reason for coming into your Bedroom, the fact is, he was there."

He paused and continued slowly:

"If he was seen to be there, you know, my dear child, as well as I do, that every door in the Social World will be closed against you."

He waited a moment before he added impressively:

"I cannot allow that to happen to my daughter any more than I can allow such a stigma to be attached to our family name."

There was silence, and then Imilda said in a broken little voice:

"Please . . . Papa . . . please . . . help . . . me."

"There is nothing I can do," the Earl answered. "After all, the Marquis is a very attractive man and, as every woman apparently is in love with him, I cannot believe you are the exception. He may have a reputation as a womaniser, but a lot of men have that and still become very happily married."

He walked across the room to his desk.

"Personally," he said as he sat down, "I think things might be far worse, and quite frankly, I am delighted to have such an excellent rider as my son-in-law."

Imilda jumped up from the chair in which she was sitting and went towards the door.

As she reached it, she burst into tears.

Then the Earl heard her running up the stairs to her Bedroom.

He sighed because he was very fond of his daughter.

Then he picked up his pen.

The Marquis had asked him to send an announcement of their engagement to the *London Gazette*.

As he started to write:

"The Earl of Harsbourne has much pleasure . . ." he thought to himself:

'Things might be much worse—very much worse.'

chapter three

IMILDA did not cry for very long.

But she felt as if she were sitting in darkness and there was no light to show her the way out.

She stayed in her room for a time.

Then she put on her riding-clothes and went to the Stables.

She had one horse which she loved more than any others.

Apollo was all black except for a star on his nose.

He started moving about his stall the moment he heard her come into the yard.

She told one of the Stable-boys to saddle him.

Then she rode off alone, going into the woods, where she took all her troubles.

There was something she always thought magical about the dimness of them with the sun sliding through the leaves.

They cast a pattern of gold on the mossy paths.

She loved the sound of the rabbits moving in the

undergrowth and the birds nesting in the boughs above.

Now she would have to leave the woods behind if she married the Marquis.

He would want to spend most of the time in London.

"I cannot do it! I will . . . not do . . . it!"

She said the words over and over again.

At the same time, she knew that every possible pressure would be put upon her to marry him.

The most effective of all was her Father's warning that to refuse would put a stigma on his name.

She rode on, moving slowly between the trees.

She saw nothing of the beauty which had always thrilled her.

She could only see the long years ahead with a man who she was quite certain did not even like her.

Of course he preferred the beautiful and sophisticated women he could flirt with and who had a language of their own.

Imilda came to the conclusion that the only thing they had in common was that they both loved horses.

Yet the Marquis was hardly likely to be interested in how a young girl rode, when he himself was such an exceptional rider.

It was a very slight bond on which to base a successful marriage.

She rode on and on until *Apollo* was getting tired and she knew she must return.

That in itself was misery.

She was quite certain her Stepmother would be looking triumphant.

Her Father would be slightly apologetic and at the same time pleased, as he had said, at having the Marquis as his son-in-law.

'What can...I do? What can I...do?'' Imilda asked again.

She asked the same question of the portraits of her ancestors as she walked into the hall.

They had been through many trials and tribulations but had somehow survived.

Many of them had been outstanding Statesmen and amongst them two exceptionally successful Prime Ministers.

As Imilda went up to her Bedroom to change, she felt as if they were telling her she must not be defeated.

The Bournes had suffered in many ways, but had never lost their pride or their courage.

The majority of them had ended up respected, admired, even heroic.

There was no-one in her Bedroom, but she did not ring the bell for Betsy.

Instead, she changed very slowly into one of her attractive gowns.

As she looked at herself in the mirror, she said:

'Are you going to fight for what you want and what is right, or are you going to give in?'

It was almost as if someone else rather than herself were asking the question.

Her whole being was rebelling against being manipulated by her Stepmother and marrying a man she did not love.

Then suddenly she felt as if she were being supported by a Power greater than herself.

Her misery and despondency began to fade away.

Her brain began to work like an efficient machine.

It told her she had to find a way, a way out of this trap which not only held her fast but also the Marquis.

Imilda went into the Drawing-Room to find both her Father and Stepmother there.

They stopped talking the minute she entered and looked up at her a little apprehensively.

She knew they had been discussing what had happened and what the future held for her.

Her father rose from the chair in which he had been sitting to stand in front of the fireplace.

"I suppose you have been riding, Imilda," he said.

"It is lovely in the woods, Papa," she replied, "and I did not hurry *Apollo*, so we are neither of us overtired."

"You had better rest while you have the chance," her Stepmother said. "I have been discussing our plans with your Father and I think we should return to London the day after tomorrow. I want to give several parties which I had already planned, and now, of course, we shall have to entertain the Marquis's family and get your trousseau."

She was speaking in a hard voice, and at the same time firmly, as if she expected Imilda to argue with her.

But Imilda said nothing.

She felt as if her brain had taken control and was advising her not to be emotional, in fact, not to show her feelings in any way.

She looked at the newspapers which were lying on a stool in front of the fire and said:

"I am sure, Stepmama, all your parties will be reported in the Court columns."

"And, of course, your wedding," the Countess replied, "will be undoubtedly one of the most important occasions of the whole Season."

There was an element of delight in her voice which she could not control.

For a moment Imilda wanted to spring to her feet and scream that she would not do it.

She would not walk up the aisle on her Father's arm, knowing that most of the women in the congregation were thinking she had been clever to "catch" him.

Until now he had managed to avoid marriage and had openly laughed at the idea.

As if her Father was anxious to be conciliatory and thought his wife was being somewhat provocative, the Earl said:

"I was thinking, my Dearest, that what you would like more than anything else for a wedding-present would be one or two really spectacular horses! We will go to Tattersall's Sale Rooms to see what they have to offer."

"Thank you, Papa," Imilda replied, "but all I really want to have with me wherever I go is *Apollo*."

The Earl smiled.

"I thought you would say that, and there will be plenty of room for him in the Marquis's Stables both in London and at Newmarket, where I understand he has some outstanding race-horses."

Imilda was just about to say that it seemed extraordinary that he did not keep the horses he rode at Melverley.

Then, almost as if someone were prompting her, she had an idea!

At the back of her mind, as she rode through the woods, had been a thought that she should run away.

The difficulty was to find a hiding-place where she could take *Apollo* with her.

It was impossible to think of being anywhere without him.

At the same time, he was very conspicuous.

If anyone was looking for her on a jet black horse with a white star on his nose, she would not be able to hide for very long.

She had had to dismiss such a plan as being impossible.

Now suddenly she had the answer.

It was only with difficulty she did not greet it with a shout of joy.

Dinner was a rather uncomfortable meal.

The Earl did his best to placate his daughter.

The Countess found it impossible to disguise the fact that she was delighted at the thought of her Stepdaughter making such a brilliant marriage.

A marriage which would undoubtedly open for her, too, some doors she had thought it impossible to enter.

When dinner was over, Imilda said she was going to retire to bed.

"I think that is a good idea," the Earl said. "I have a great deal to see to on the Estate before we leave for London."

He paused a moment and then continued:

"If you would like to ride with me about eleven o'clock, we will go over to Johnson's Farm first, as I have to see him about various things."

"I would love to go with you, Papa," Imilda answered. "I will be ready at eleven and not keep you waiting."

"That is my girl," the Earl said as he kissed her.

"You must enjoy your freedom while you can," the Countess said.

It was as if she could not help saying something which she knew would hurt her Stepdaughter.

"Goodnight, Stepmama," Imilda replied.

Because she was determined to have her say, the Countess continued:

"Of course we do not know how soon the Marquis wishes to be married, but we should start getting your trousseau the moment we reach London. In my opinion, it should take place in a month's time."

Imilda did not deign to answer.

She knew only too well that her Stepmother was "rubbing salt in the wound."

Once again it made her want to scream that she would not do it.

Instead, she went quietly upstairs to lie, for a long time, planning step by step what she would do.

She went riding with her Father the next morning.

She made it for herself a very important occasion, because it would be a long time before she rode with him again.

They talked of things she had done when she was a child.

The Earl pointed out to her improvements he was making on the Estate.

Now that the war had ended, new agricultural machinery was being made for farming.

"I intend to increase my livestock," the Earl said, "as I think they will be more saleable than crops."

"Are the farmers still being undercut by food imported from the continent?" Imilda enquired.

She wanted to make sure that what she had said to the Marquis was correct.

"I am afraid the farmers are still having a very thin time," the Earl replied. "That is why we must cultivate produce which can be sold cheaper than what comes in from abroad."

Imilda listened, as she always did, to everything her Father told her, and especially on this occasion, since she did not know when they would ride together again.

When they got back to the house, it was to find there was already a pile of trunks in the hall which had been packed on her Stepmother's orders.

"You look as if you are taking half the house with you," the Earl said jokingly.

"If we are to stay in London until the end of the Season," the Countess replied, "I shall need everything I possess already and a great deal more."

"I shall have to come back here from time to time," the Earl said. "You know as well as I do, there is a great deal to be seen to on the Estate."

"It is one thing for you to slip down on your own," the Countess replied, "but quite another for me to come with you. And I am sure Imilda will be busy enjoying the many parties which will be given for her and her *fiancé*."

The Countess said the last two words in an affected manner.

It made Imilda clench her fingers together.

She knew only too well that her Stepmother was delighted she had been unable to make any further protest against the marriage.

The Countess was determined to make her admit how lucky she was to have captured anyone so elusive as the Marquis of Melverley.

Imilda went up to her room.

She thought as she did so how much she hated her Stepmother.

If what she was about to do would really upset and humiliate her, she did not care.

She had already got together the things she intended to take with her when she ran away.

It was possible to attach a large bag on each side of *Apollo*'s saddles.

If carefully packed, these could carry a great deal.

There was also a place behind the saddle where a heavy coat could be attached.

Because it was now nearly summer, it was easy to pack quite a number of light gowns.

She looked at what she had already packed and added a few more things which she thought would be useful.

Her great difficulty was to provide herself with money.

This she knew was absolutely necessary in case what she had planned turned out not to be possible.

She waited until her Father and Stepmother had come up to bed.

Then she went down to the room which was used by her Father's Secretary, who was also the Manager of the Estate.

In a large safe he kept the money with which he paid the wages every Friday.

It also contained the rents he received from the tenants.

About once a month he went into St. Albans to pay them into the Bank.

As it was now within a few days of the end of April, there would be quite a large sum waiting to be transferred.

Luckily she knew where the key to the safe was kept.

It was supposed to be a secret from everyone in the house.

However, she had sometimes been there when her Father wanted money unexpectedly and had opened the safe in the absence of his Secretary.

She now crept downstairs and went into the darkened room, taking with her a candle from the sconce.

She moved very quietly even though she was quite sure there was no-one in that part of the house to hear her.

There was a large amount of money in the safe as she had expected.

She took two hundred pounds, thinking that would last her for a long time.

She then wrote an I.O.U., signed it with her name, and put it at the bottom of the pile.

Having locked the safe, she put the candle back from where she had taken it and went upstairs to bed.

Imilda had made no plans to be with her Father the next morning.

She knew he had a large number of people to see before he left for London the following day.

There were repairs to be made to one of the Stables.

A new Greenhouse to be erected in the Kitchen garden.

There was some trouble over the water feeding into the lake.

This meant there would be long consultations over what should be done in their absence.

Imilda had breakfast with her Father.

Then, as he rose to go to the Study, she said:

"Do not work too hard, Papa. But of course you want everything to be perfect here as it always is. I love my home."

"I shall miss you, my Dearest, when you have to leave it," the Earl said, "but it is just one of those things that has to happen in life."

He kissed her cheek and then, as he turned towards the door, he said:

"Oh, by the way, your engagement should be announced in the *London Gazette* this morning."

He hurried away without waiting for his daughter's reply, as if he were afraid of what she might say.

It was, however, what Imilda had expected, and she had no wish to read it.

She wanted only to get away, as she intended to do, as quickly as possible.

It was still too early for her Stepmother to be up.

Betsy and the other maids had not started to make the beds or do the rooms.

Imilda picked up the bags in which her clothes were packed.

Going downstairs by a secondary staircase, she reached the Stables without anyone seeing her.

She told one of the Stable-boys to saddle *Apollo*.

As he walked across the yard, he said:

"Oi thinks as how ye would be riding this mornin', M'Lady, and we'll miss ye when ye go to London."

"And I shall miss you," Imilda replied.

When she went into the stall carrying the bags, which were quite heavy, the Stable-boy looked at them in surprise.

"I am taking some things I do not need to someone who is ill," Imilda explained.

The lad smiled.

"That be kind o' ye, M'Lady, and just like yer Mither. 'Er was always takin' ter them that were ill or in trouble somethin' to cheer 'em up."

Imilda smiled at him and, mounting *Apollo*, she rode out of the yard.

There was no-one to see her go.

There was no need to fear that they might guess later, from the direction she took, where she had gone.

She knew the place she had chosen was beyond all

doubt the last place where they would expect to find her.

She rode across the Father's fields and passed through the woods.

Then she set out in a more or less direct line to where, near the border of the county, she knew she would find Melverley Hall.

She had never been there.

But because she had hunted with her Father, she knew exactly where it was.

In fact, last Winter she had seen it in the far distance after an exceptionally long run that had ended in her and the Earl having a very tiring ride home.

When she had been wondering where she could possibly hide, the idea had suddenly struck her.

Wherever they tried to think she might have gone, no-one would suppose for a moment that she would hide from the Marquis in his own house.

For some reason which she could not understand, he had never been home since his Father died.

When he had returned from France with the first 30,000 soldiers repatriated from the Army of Occupation, he had stayed in London.

Then he had started his series of frivolous love affairs which had caused so much sensational gossip.

Imilda was half afraid that when her Father realised she had actually left and could not be found, he might send for the Bow Street Runners.

She was, however, quite certain he would not do so unless he was desperate.

First of all, he would want to cover up her disappearance.

He would say she was too ill to come to London, or perhaps that she was visiting friends and relations who wished to hear about her engagement.

Eventually he would have to admit to himself that she was genuinely determined not to marry the Marquis.

Then he might, when every other enquiry had failed, call in professionals to search the country for her.

Again Imilda was confident that the last place they would look would be in Melverley Hall.

It would occur to no-one that she would choose such a hiding-place.

She was, at the same time, afraid that to be accepted in Melverley Hall might be more difficult than she hoped.

But she had with her a piece of paper which she thought should be effective.

It encouraged her to believe she really had been clever enough to outwit her Stepmother, who had forced the situation upon her.

It took longer than she had expected to reach the Hall, even riding across country.

She had thought it a mistake to stop for food at an Inn.

She was certain that if she were not remembered, *Apollo* would be.

She had, therefore, brought with her something to eat.

She stopped by a fresh stream running through a meadow and *Apollo* drank the water.

She ate the toast which she had saved from breakfast and had spread with butter and honey.

She had taken the plate up to her Bedroom.

Then she packed the toast in paper so that it would not make a mess in the pocket of her jacket.

She thought now it tasted very good.

She cupped her hands and drank some water from the stream.

Then they were ready to go on.

It was nearly four o'clock when she saw ahead of her Melverley Hall.

When she had seen it in the dim distance in the Winter, it was too far to see it at all clearly.

Now, as she drew nearer to it, she was impressed.

Built in the reign of Queen Elizabeth, it was in the shape of an "E" and, in the sunshine, was very lovely.

The red bricks had mellowed with the years into a soft pink.

The house itself was standing on high ground that fell away to a large lake in front of it, crossed by an ancient stone bridge.

There were white swans swimming on the lake.

As she drew nearer, a flight of white doves fluttered from the trees in the Park to settle on the lawn.

Now she could see that the house was somewhat neglected and, like the garden that surrounded it, needed attention.

At the same time, it was beautiful and she could not imagine how any man could neglect and refuse to visit so lovely a place.

She crossed the bridge.

Then she rode *Apollo* round to the back of the house, where she expected the Stables would be.

She found them, and while they, too, were picturesque, she saw a number of tiles were missing from the roofs.

Even the cobbled yard needed repair.

It appeared at first as if no-one was about.

Then an elderly man with grey hair appeared.

"Be ye lookin' for some'un?" he asked.

"I am looking for a stall in which to put my horse," Imilda replied.

He looked at her in surprise. Then he asked:

"Be yer visiting someun' in th' house?"

"I am hoping that I shall be staying here," Imilda answered.

He now looked at her in astonishment, and she said:

"This is *Apollo*, and we have come a long way. So I would be grateful if you would give him something to eat and drink."

The man hesitated.

Then he obviously thought it was not his business to argue with a visitor.

He took *Apollo*'s rein and drew him inside a Stable.

For a moment Imilda was half afraid it might be very rough.

However, to her relief, she saw the first stall they came to had fresh straw in it.

There was also a pail filled with clean water.

She waited while the man removed *Apollo*'s saddle, then took off his bridle and patted him.

He moved quickly towards the manger.

She was glad to see there were fresh oats in it and also some hay.

She looked at the other stalls, and there were quite a number of them.

She could see that they, too, had been bedded down with fresh straw.

There were no horses, but certainly the stalls were ready for them if or when they came.

"Thank you, thank you very much," she said to the elderly man.

Then before she walked away, she paused to say:

"Can you tell me who is the Manager here in

charge of the Estate, or perhaps it is a Secretary who runs it?"

The elderly man thought for a moment, then scratched his head.

"That be Mr. Richardson," he said, "but 'e be ill and in 'is cottage."

Imilda drew in her breath.

This was something she had not expected.

Then she told herself there must be someone in authority.

Without asking any more questions, she walked towards the house.

She knocked at the back-door, which was ajar, and as no-one answered, she walked in.

There was the usual long passage with larders on either side of it, just as there were at her own home.

She passed the Kitchen, which seemed very quiet.

There was no-one there, and she saw on the far side of it the Servants' Hall.

It was a large room and appeared comfortably furnished, but it, too, was empty.

She began to think that the Marquis had deserted his home and there was no-one left in it.

Then, as she came to the pantry, she heard voices.

As she neared it, a man came out.

He was an elderly man with a certain look of authority, and she was sure he must be the Butler.

He looked at her in surprise, and she said:

"Good afternoon. I have come with a message from the Marquis of Melverley for Mr. Richardson, but I understand he is ill."

"A message from His Lordship?" the man facing her said.

He was obviously astonished, and Imilda said:

"Yes, indeed, and perhaps if Mr. Richardson is ill,

then you will be able to tell me what to do."

As she spoke, she took from her pocket a note she had put into an unaddressed envelope.

She had written on a piece of plain white vellum paper:

"This is to introduce Miss Graham, who is to take over the care of the Herb Garden.

"Kindly accommodate her in the house and see that she has any help she requires in the garden."

The paper was signed "Melverley."

Imilda had copied his signature carefully from the visitors' book at home.

She had done it very skilfully, and it was impossible for anyone to suspect it was a forgery.

The Butler took it and read it very slowly.

Then he said in a voice which showed he was exceedingly surprised:

"His Lordship wants you to take over the Herb Garden?"

"Yes," Imilda replied. "I understand it is somewhat neglected."

She had been afraid that there might not be an Herb Garden at Melverley Hall at all.

But she assured herself, as it was an Elizabethan House, it must in those days have had a Herb Garden.

She was quite sure it would have continued to be in existence up to the time of the last Marquis's death.

She knew a great deal, as it happened, about Herb Gardens.

She thought it was clever of her to have thought of a position which would not interfere with anyone else.

It would also give her the shelter of Melverley Hall,

where no-one would find her.

The Butler looked at the paper again as if he could not believe it.

Then he said:

"I don't know about this, I really don't!"

"That is what His Lordship wants," Imilda said firmly, "and it is unfortunate he did not know that Mr. Richardson is ill."

"We'll have to do what we can," the Butler said with an effort.

"Thank you," Imilda replied. "I have put my horse in the Stables and I would be grateful if you would show me where I can sleep so that I can put down my luggage."

She was carrying the bags which were very heavy.

As if he were suddenly aware of it, the Butler reached forwards to take one from her.

"I thinks," he said, "you'd be best upstairs with Nanny."

Imilda's eyes opened wider, and she said quickly:

"So you have a Nanny here! I would love to be with her. I am sure she is in the Nursery."

"That's right," the Butler said, "where her's always been. It's her home, so to speak."

It was almost, Imilda thought, as if he were apologising for her being there.

The Butler turned and walked along the corridor, and Imilda followed him.

He came to a small staircase and started up it.

Imilda could not help noticing that while it was not positively dirty, there was a great deal of dust which should have been removed.

The Butler moved slowly because he was obviously an old man.

Imilda suspected his feet hurt him.

They rested for a moment when they got to the first floor, and she said:

"I suppose, because His Lordship is in London, you are short-handed."

"Yes, that be so, we be short-handed," the Butler agreed.

He did not seem to want to say any more and started up the next flight of stairs which led to the second floor.

Imilda was afraid that the Nursery might be higher still.

To her relief, they turned left and walked to what she knew was the East Wing.

There was a door in front of them, and the Butler knocked on it.

A voice said:

"Come in!"

When he opened the door, Imilda saw a Nursery which was almost a replica of her own.

There was a rocking-horse against one wall which had lost its tail.

A screen covered with Christmas cards stuck over it, stood on one side of the fireplace.

Opposite, seated in a rocking-chair, was an elderly woman.

"Good afternoon, Mr. Hutton," she said, "I am surprised to see you up so high."

"I have brought you someone who has come on His Lordship's instructions," the Butler said, "to look after the Herb Garden."

"On His Lordship's instructions!" the old woman exclaimed.

"Yes, Nanny. He's written to say she's to be in charge of the Herb Garden and sleep in the house. So I thinks it'd be wise to bring her to you."

"Very sensible, Mr. Hutton," Nanny replied.

With some difficulty, she rose to her feet.

Then, as Imilda came forward, she held out her hand.

"It is nice to see you, Miss . . ."

She paused to look at the Butler.

"Miss Graham," the Butler said quickly. "That's what His Lordship says."

"I should love to be with you," Imilda said, "that is, if you will have me. I had a Nanny of my own and I was always happy with her."

"Of course you were, dear," Nanny said as she smiled. "Is that your luggage?"

She looked at the bag Imilda held in her hand and the one the Butler was carrying.

"I came on horseback," Imilda explained. "I have put *Apollo* in the Stables."

To her surprise, the Butler and Nanny exchanged glances.

Then he said:

"In that case they 'ave to know."

"She'll be all right with me," Nanny said. "I'll look after her."

"They may not like it," the Butler said almost beneath his breath.

"If 'tis His Lordship's orders, there's nothing they can do about it. Now, don't you worry, Mr. Hutton. Just say that Miss Graham'll have her food upstairs here with me."

"It seems strange," the Butler said, "him sending her like that, and not a word have we heard from him these last six months."

"Now, don't fuss," Nanny said, "you knows it's bad for your arthritis."

"What about . . .'er?" Mr. Hutton enquired.

"Just tell her Miss Graham is up here and she'll be no trouble to no-one."

The Butler put down on one of the chairs the bag he was carrying.

Then, shaking his head as if he were worried, he walked towards the door.

Imilda expected him to speak to her, but he left without a word.

Only when the door closed behind him did Nanny say:

"You've given them all a shock. We haven't heard from His Lordship for months and months, and now he's sent you to look after the Herb Garden. He has certainly set you a task."

"Is it in a bad state?" Imilda asked.

"Full of weeds," Nanny said. "Her Ladyship would turn in her grave if she saw it, that she would."

Imilda smiled.

"I was sure that the Marquis's Mother would have cared for the Herb Garden just like my own Mother cared for ours."

She thought rather bitterly as she spoke that her Stepmother had never taken the slightest interest in the herbs.

Although the gardens were perfectly kept, there was no-one but herself to go into them now, no-one to make medicines for those who were ill in the village, as her Mother had always done.

"Now, sit down," Nanny was saying. "I expects you would like a cup of tea."

"I would love one," Imilda answered. "But not if it is any trouble."

"I makes my own tea, you can be sure of that," Nanny said. "It's difficult to get it out of them downstairs. They always want to give me coffee 'cos it's cheaper, but I make sure I have my tea."

Imilda thought with a smile that it might be her old Nanny speaking.

When she died five years ago, she had been miserable.

In fact, she had never gone up to the Nursery again because the memory made her so unhappy.

There was something about this large Nursery which made her feel she had come home.

She could see a large Teddy bear in one corner.

There was a fort against one wall with tin soldiers arranged on the Parade Ground.

Imilda had owned a Doll's House, but this was a boy's Nursery.

As a child the Marquis would have played with a fort and soldiers, and she expected there were pop-guns somewhere in the room.

Although it was a warm day, Nanny had a fire.

The kettle she put on it was soon boiling.

There were cups, saucers, and a tin containing biscuits on a chest of drawers.

Nanny poured out the tea, adding milk and sugar without asking Imilda what she wanted.

She brought it over to the chair in which she was sitting.

"Thank you," Imilda said, "thank you very much."

Nanny offered her the biscuits, which were actually shortcakes.

As she was hungry, she had two and then had a third when Nanny offered them again.

"Now, tell me about yourself," Nanny was saying. "It's exciting for me to have a visitor, I can tell you that."

"There seem to be very few people in the house," Imilda said.

"Oh, there's plenty at times, but not always what one wants," Nanny said in a slightly strange tone of voice. "In fact, I must tell you, Miss Graham, it's best to shut your eyes and see nothing, close your lips and say nothing."

Imilda did not understand.

Yet there was a note in Nanny's voice which told her she was serious.

'I will do whatever you say," she replied. "I want to stay here because I need employment desperately."

"I suppose your parents are dead," Nanny said. "That happens to us all, and then we finds ourselves alone. But it often breaks your heart."

"I felt mine was broken when my Mother died," Imilda said, "and things have never been the same since."

"No, of course not," Nanny agreed. "But you'll be happy enough here if you just keeps yourself to yourself."

"I will do whatever you tell me." Imilda smiled.

At the same time, she wondered what the mystery was about.

"It is a very beautiful house," she said.

"It was," Nanny replied. "It was so lovely that people came from all over the county to see it, and Her Ladyship gave parties which made everyone who came to them happy."

"That is what a party is for," Imilda said.

"I can see that you and I think the same," Nanny said, "and I'll say again, Miss Graham, it's nice to have you."

Imilda had chosen the name Graham because it was the name of one of her Governesses.

She thought that if anyone did happen to ask for her Christian name, she would say it was Milly.

It was not too unlike her own.

"You might easily be one of my children," Nanny was saying, "and I miss them more than I can say."

She gave a deep sigh.

"I always hoped that Master Vulcan would marry and I'd have his son to care for. But after he went off to that wicked war, I'm afraid it changed him. As you can see, the Nursery's empty."

"It is a very beautiful Nursery," Imilda said, "and very like my own."

"I guessed as soon as I sees you that you'd been brought up proper," Nanny said. "You're a Lady and this is no place for a Lady at the moment, I can tell you that."

"Why?" Imilda asked.

She wondered if Nanny would tell her the truth, but thought it unlikely.

She was right, because Nanny said quickly:

"You'll learn about things sooner or later, and the later the better. Just you remember to keep your eyes open and your mouth shut. That is all I can say to you."

This, naturally, made Imilda more curious than ever.

She finished her tea and Nanny showed her a Bedroom.

It had been, she said, the Marquis's when he was a baby in the cradle.

It was his again as a boy.

It was the sort of room that a boy would have.

There were his special treasures just as William had them in his Bedroom at home.

Large shells he had found at some time on a seashore were to be seen.

Also drawings of horses, some by himself and some by an artist.

His first gun hung on the wall over the bed, and there were a number of ancient swords which he had collected.

He had been given them as presents at Christmas and on his birthdays.

The room had a large and comfortable-looking bed which Imilda thought was more important than anything else.

She took off her riding-clothes and put on a comfortable gown.

It was pretty but simple and actually was one she had worn at school.

It was dinner-time when she went back to the Nursery.

Nanny looked at the clock.

"I'm supposed to have my dinner at seven o'clock," she said, "but if they're late, it is often an hour or more before it comes upstairs."

Imilda badly wanted to know who "they" were.

But she realised Nanny had said it without meaning to, so she let it pass.

She was, however, getting more and more curious about what was going on in the house.

Why were there eight stalls, clean and ready for horses that were not there?

There was something very strange going on, Imilda told herself.

She felt she must find out the truth, or she would puzzle and puzzle, and doubtless be unable to sleep.

"I suppose," she said casually, because it had just occurred to her, "that it is too late for me to go and look at the Herb Garden."

Nanny made a sound which was almost a cry.

"At this time of night?" she exclaimed. "You stay here with me! It's the last thing you should be doing, walking about the house or the garden after six o'clock."

"But why . . . ?" Imilda began.

As she spoke, the door opened.

A woman came in who looked about thirty-five or forty.

She appeared at first sight to be a Senior servant of some sort.

Then, as she came further into the room, Imilda saw to her astonishment that her face was painted, not discreetly, but with a bright touch of rouge on her cheeks, red lips, and undoubtedly mascaraed eyelashes.

"Now what's going on up here?" she asked, looking at Nanny.

"Good evening, Mrs. Gibbons," Nanny replied. "I expect you've heard that His Lordship has sent Miss Graham, whom you see here, to look after the Herb Garden."

"And why should His Lordship do that, I'd like to know," Mrs. Gibbons said in a hostile voice.

"It's nothing to do with me, I can assure you," Nanny replied. "Perhaps he was thinking of his dead Mother and how fond she was of it."

"Whatever he was thinking," Mrs. Gibbons said, "it is, as you're well aware, most inconvenient. We've no place for strangers here, and I think, Miss Graham, you'd be well advised to look elsewhere for employment."

Imilda rose from the chair in which she was sitting.

She held out her hand and said:

"I am sorry if I have caused any trouble. His Lordship was most insistent that I should come here, and

I think he would be upset and disappointed if I did not stay."

There was a silence, and then Nanny said:

"His Lordship might come down to find out why Miss Graham was unwilling to do what he wanted."

To Imilda's surprise, Mrs. Gibbons seemed upset at this suggestion.

She stared at Nanny, and if she had not been so painted, Imilda had the idea that she might have gone pale.

Then she said:

"But of course we're very pleased to have Miss Graham, and I'm sure she'll improve the garden, which is in a very bad state, very bad indeed!"

"I will do my best," Imilda said quietly.

"And I hope you'll be comfortable up here with Nanny," Mrs. Gibbons said. "It'd be a great mistake to go walking about the house at night. You might see a ghost or two. There are plenty in this house, I promise you that."

"I am sure there are," Imilda said. "Old houses are always the same. I lived in one before and I know they can be very creepy."

"That's the right word," Mrs. Gibbons approved, "and unless you want to feel frightened, Miss Graham, you stay here with Nanny."

She paused a moment before she continued:

"You are safe with her, and when you go down in the morning, just go straight out of the front-door and you'll find the Herb Garden on the left-hand side of the lawn."

"Thank you very much," Imilda said. "Could a Gardener meet me there? I would like to tell him what I shall want in the way of tools."

"I'll tell him to be there at nine-thirty," Mrs. Gibbons said. "As I have said, straight out the front-door and across the lawn to the left."

"I am sure I shall find it," Imilda said, "and thank you very much for your help."

Mrs. Gibbons looked across the room at Nanny.

There was a warning in her face and her voice as she said:

"You look after her, Nanny, and see she doesn't get into mischief. It's quite easy to get lost in this house, as you well knows."

"She'll be all right with me," Nanny promised.

chapter four

IMILDA woke early but there was no sound of breakfast until nearly nine o'clock.

She longed to go to the Stables to see *Apollo*, but she thought it would be rude on her first morning to go without discussing it with Nanny.

When she had finished breakfast, Nanny reminded her that the Gardener was waiting for her at nine-thirty in the Herb Garden.

She also reiterated the instructions Mrs. Gibbons had given her.

It seemed to Imilda extraordinary that there was so much fuss about her finding her way to the garden.

As it was her first day, she did exactly as she was told.

She went down the main staircase into the hall and found the Herb Garden quite easily.

An elderly Gardener was there waiting for her, and she shook his hand, saying:

"I expect you have been told I have come on His

Lordship's instructions to attend to this garden."

"Oi be afraid it's run wild, Miss," the Gardener replied. "We be short-handed, and 'tis only with difficulty us can provide enough fruit an' vegetables for th' house."

Imilda felt that not much could be required, as there seemed so few people living in it.

However, she thought it would be a mistake to ask the Gardener questions except about the garden.

He showed her round.

She saw with dismay that the herbs which had been there were now lost amongst the weeds and nettles.

The paths also were in a bad state.

"I suppose," she said, "you could not spare me a boy to clean the paths. I will weed as much as I can of the garden, but paths take a long time, and I think if we are not careful, we shall lose a lot of plants."

"Oi be thinkin' that m'self," the Gardener said. "Oi'll fine ye a lad, but as Oi be sayin', we be short-handed."

He gave her a spade, a trowel, and a pitch-fork which she thought would be too heavy for her.

However, she accepted everything he brought with him.

Then he showed her a little shed in the corner of the garden where they could be stored.

It seemed to Imilda that he had no wish to be conversational, and he left her alone.

She thought with a sigh she had certainly set herself a Herculean task.

The Herb Garden, when it had been properly looked after, must have been a delightful sight.

It was surrounded by Elizabethian brick walls.

An elegant gateway led into the garden and in the centre of it there was a small fountain.

It was not as large as the fountain in the centre of the lawn.

It was, however, elegantly carved with a small cupid holding a fish with the water flowing out of its mouth.

There had once been water lillies in the bowl, but they had died.

Imilda thought they should be replaced.

It struck her that she had no idea who to ask what money she could spend on the garden.

She had assumed that when she came to Melverley there would be a Secretary or Manager.

He would be a man such as her Father had at home, who would take charge of the wages and all expenses.

Unfortunately, the man who should do that here was ill, and there was no-one else to turn to for her requirements.

It all seemed very strange.

Yet she supposed that, even if the Marquis did not come home, he provided money for the wages of the servants who were still there.

She worked in the garden until nearly twelve o'clock.

She then decided she must see *Apollo*.

She put the tools the Gardener had given her tidily away in the shed and walked across the lawn.

It was easy to find a path through a mass of shrubs which led her to the Stables.

They seemed as deserted as they had when she arrived the previous afternoon.

She went into the Stable where she had left *Apollo* and saw with a sense of shock that he was not in the stall.

The stall had, however, been used.

When she looked down the row, to her surprise she

saw that the other stalls had also been used.

She looked at them in bewilderment.

She was absolutely certain that when she had seen them yesterday, they were fresh and unused.

She walked down the passage and looked into each stall.

It was clear that a horse had been in each one the previous night.

"I do not understand," Imilda murmured.

Then a voice from the doorway said:

"Oh, there ye be, Miss. Oi 'spect ye be lookin' for yer horse."

"Yes, I am," Imilda said. "Where is *Apollo*?"

It was the old man who had looked after her yesterday.

He beckoned with his finger and she walked quickly towards him.

"As Oi learns ye be workin' here," he said, "Oi put yer horse in with th' others."

He did not wait for a reply but went ahead into the next Stable.

There, to Imilda's relief, she saw *Apollo* in the first stall.

He whinnied when he saw her.

She opened the door, patted him, and he nuzzled against her.

"We will go riding this afternoon," she said.

"He's been comfortable in here," the old man said, "and as ye can see, 'e 'as company."

Imilda looked at the other stalls and saw they housed five horses.

Without asking the old man's permission, she began to inspect them.

Three of the horses were obviously old and must, she thought, have belonged to the Marquis's Father.

There were also two young horses.

As she patted them, the old man said:

"They'll be fine next year, but as things be, they don't 'ave proper exercise."

"I will exercise them," Imilda said eagerly, "but of course *Apollo* must come first."

"I 'oped ye'd say that, Miss."

"I tell you what I will do," Imilda said. "I will take *Apollo* for a ride immediately after luncheon, and when I come back, if you saddle one of these young horses for me, I will ride him round the paddock."

"That be real kind o' ye," the old man said. "They don't get enough attention, an' that be th' truth."

"Are these all the horses that His Lordship possesses?" Imilda asked.

The old man parted his lips as if to speak and then shut them again.

She realised she had asked a question he had no wish to answer.

There was an uncomfortable silence, and then Imilda said:

"I will go back now and change into my riding-clothes. It would be very kind of you if you would saddle *Apollo* for me."

"I'll do that, Miss," the old man replied.

She hurried back into the house.

Here was another puzzle, she thought, to which she had no answer.

Who used the horses in the other Stable to which she had first taken *Apollo*?

Why were there apparently so few horses belonging to the Marquis?

Unless, of course, he had recently sold some.

But if he had, surely the old man would have said so.

The most pressing question of all was—who had used the eight stalls last night which were now empty?

"I have to know the answer to all these questions sooner or later," Imilda told herself.

She had the feeling that Nanny would not want to answer them.

When she reached the Nursery, she found Nanny was waiting for her.

Luncheon was already on the table.

"Is everything all right?" Nanny asked.

"Yes, perfectly all right, except there is a great deal of work to do," Imilda replied. "I think it would take me years to get the Herb Garden looking as it must have looked when His Lordship was a boy."

Nanny sighed.

"Those were the days, and a nicer young Gentleman I've never known than Master Vulcan."

"Tell me about him," Imilda said as she sat down at the table.

She felt that Nanny was only too ready to talk about the old days.

"Why are people so unhappy here?" she asked halfway through the meal. "Why has he not come back since he returned from the war?"

"Everything was changed," Nanny answered, "When Her Ladyship died and His Lordship married again."

"Then the Marquis has a Stepmother?" Imilda exclaimed.

"She hated my baby from the moment she came into the house," Nanny went on. "She was jealous of him, that's what it was. She tried to put his Father against him and everyone else who would listen to her."

"How terrible!" Imilda said. "How old was His Lordship when this happened?"

"He was thirteen when Her Ladyship died and there was not a person on the Estate that did not cry at the loss of her. Yet His Lordship married again."

She sighed before she went on:

"He was lonely, and that's the truth. She was determined to get him. She wanted to be a Marchioness, and when she got what she wanted, she made this house miserable for everyone in it."

Imilda was beginning to understand why the Marquis did not want to come home.

Nanny went on to tell her of how his Stepmother had mentally tortured him by finding fault with everything he did.

"Even when he was old enough to go to Oxford." Nanny said, "he would come up here and tell me how unhappy he was. It be wrong to speak ill of the dead, but she made Master Vulcan's life a Hell, which is where I hope she is by now."

The way she spoke was very moving.

Imilda could not help thinking how cruel it had been for a small boy to be confronted by a Stepmother even worse than her own.

Nanny had bottled it all up inside her for a long time.

She was therefore only too willing to tell of the miseries they had all suffered under a new mistress.

"Did the Marquis resent what she was doing?" Imilda asked when Nanny paused for breath.

"He wanted the peace and quiet he had had with the wife he loved," Nanny answered, "and of course Her new Ladyship was all honey and cream where he was concerned. She flattered him, talked to him in a soft voice, and pretended that every change she was making was just to increase his comfort."

Nanny's voice sharpened as she went on:

"Only we and Master Vulcan got the rough side of her tongue! She raged at the servants until the women were in tears, and the men, if they could afford it, gave in their notice."

"She must have been a horrible woman," Imilda said. "When did she die?"

"Only two years ago, when His Lordship was in France," Nanny answered. "Mr. Richardson informed him that she was dead. A heart attack, the Doctors called it, and he arranged the Funeral."

She sighed.

"There was no message from His Lordship, and I knew in my bones he wouldn't be coming back here if he could help it."

"It seems such a pity," Imilda said, "when it is such a lovely house."

"It was a lovely house," Nanny said, emphasising the word. "Things are not what they ought to be, and I've asked myself over and over again what I can do."

There was a little pause, and then Imilda said:

"Why not tell me what is wrong?"

It was quite a simple question, but it seemed to startle Nanny.

She got up from the table, saying:

"Now, don't you worry your head about things that don't concern you. Just you keep to the Herb Garden and your horse, and everything'll be all right."

Imilda thought that was very unlikely, but she did not want to argue.

She changed quickly into her riding-habit and hurried to the Stables.

Apollo was waiting for her.

She took him just to the paddocks, which needed attention but at one time must have been exceptional.

Then she went through the woods.

They were very like the woods at home which she loved.

She thought that however difficult things might be in the house, she would always find peace here.

She remembered she had promised to exercise one of the other horses and took *Apollo* back to the Stables.

She thought he looked at her reproachfully when she mounted the young horse that the old man had ready for her.

It was a good thing she was an experienced rider.

The young horse she found had hardly been broken in.

He started off bucking and kicking and showing his independence.

Finally she got him out of the yard and into the paddock.

By the time she had taken him round two or three times, he was responding to what she wanted.

In fact, he was enjoying himself.

The old man had stood at the gate, watching her, and when she rode back to him he said:

"Ye be a fine rider, Miss, an' there's no mistake about that."

"I think this is a very nice horse," Imilda said, "but of course he should be ridden regularly, every day if possible."

"I knows that," the old man said, "but Oi have too much to do an' only one boy to help me. He be getting some fresh straw now an' he ain't too quick about anythin' he does."

"I will ride the other young horse tomorrow," Imilda promised. "But please look after *Apollo* for me."

"Ye can be sure Oi'll do that, Miss," the old man replied.

She realised as she walked back to the house that it was after half-past four and Nanny would be waiting for her tea.

There was no-one in the hall when she let herself in.

She suddenly remembered that she wanted something to read.

She knew there were only children's books in the Nursery.

As she loved reading, it would be impossible for her to go on day after day without books.

'I am quite certain this lovely house has a Library,' she thought.

Instead of going up the stairs, she walked along a passage from the hall.

She peeped into the rooms as she passed, until at the far end she found what she was seeking.

It was a very impressive library and exactly what Imilda thought such a beautiful house should have.

It was excellently planned.

The rail of the Balcony was made of bronze in a heavy but attractive pattern which Imilda had not seen before.

She thought it might have been added to the Library some time in the Sixteenth Century.

She could not resist climbing up the spiral steps and going on to the Balcony.

She was rewarded when she found that books of the kind she wanted were there.

She discovered three which she particuarly wanted to read.

She was just seeking a fourth, when she heard

someone outside the Library door.

Instinctively, because she knew after what Mrs. Gibbons had said that she should not be in this part of the house, she crouched down.

She thought perhaps it was one of the servants coming to draw the curtains.

At the moment, the afternoon sunshine was pouring through the long but small-paned windows.

Then, as she peeped through an aperture in the bronze design, she saw a man come into the Library.

He shut the door carefully behind him.

He was carrying something in one hand, and Imilda was suddenly afraid he was bringing back a book.

If so, she might have to explain to him why she was helping herself without permission.

Before he passed the small aperture through which she was looking, she saw that he was in riding-clothes, with breeches and boots.

If he put the book he was carrying back on one of the lower shelves, she thought he need never know that she was on the Balcony above him.

As she drew in her breath hopefully, she heard a click and then there was silence.

She wondered what he was doing.

Moving very carefully, she looked through another gap in the pattern of leaves that embellished the rail of the Balcony.

There was no-one in sight.

It was so extraordinary that Imilda could not believe it.

She moved again, but there was no sign anywhere of the man she had just seen come into the Library.

She was now crouching just opposite the mantel-piece.

It was exquisitely carved and had above it a portrait

which looked like a Holbein.

But where was the man?

How could he have vanished in such an extraordinary way?

She was just about to stand up and go down the spiral steps, when she heard the Library door open again.

Peeping with difficulty to see what was happening, she saw that another man had come into the room.

He, too, was shutting the door carefully behind him.

Then, as he walked forward, he said in a rather coarse voice:

"These 'ere diamonds should get a good price from old Isaacs."

For a moment Imilda thought in astonishment that he must be speaking to her.

Then she realised the first man she had lost sight of was now standing in front of the mantelpiece.

"Yer've been lucky, old boy!" he said. "But what I got with some difficulty should be worth a few gold goblins."

"Yer're always lucky, Bill," said the man who had just come in. "I'll stick this in with the rest, then us'll have a drink. I needs it."

"So do I," Bill answered, "I had some tough opposition today. I had to knock 'im about a bit."

The newcomer seemed to stiffen.

"Now, yer be careful, Bill," he said. "If yer do too much damage, they'll send the soldiers after yer, and that's somethin' none of us wants."

"Nor do I," Bill said. "But he had a pistol on him which I didn't expect."

The other man did not answer.

To Imilda's astonishment, she saw him disappear

through a panel beside the mantelpiece.

Bill must have left it open when he came back, because she had not noticed it before she climbed up onto the Balcony.

She was, however, holding her breath because she was frightened.

Bill was fidgeting about down below as he waited for the other man to return.

Imilda was terrified that he might take it in his head to climb up the spiral stairs to the Balcony.

With a sense of relief she heard the other man say:

"Well, yer an' I 'ave certainly added to the collection. I wonders what the others 'ave got."

He stepped out of the open panel and shut it behind him with a slight click.

"Let's go an' find 'em," Bill said. "If they 'aven't got much, then the laugh's on them."

"We usually get more than th' others," the other man murmured.

He and Bill walked across the Library to the door.

They passed through it and shut it behind them.

Imilda felt she could breathe again.

She now knew the answer to what had puzzled her, and it was very frightening.

The men who were living in the house and kept their horses in the Stables were Highwaymen.

It was quite obvious that what they were hiding in the secret passage was their ill-gotten gains from helpless travellers.

These they would later sell to Isaacs, whoever he might be.

Imilda now understood why no-one wanted a stranger in Melverley.

Mrs. Gibbons had warned her not to go wandering about the house.

She picked up the books.

She knew she must get back to Nanny before any of the other men came to deposit what they had stolen.

She climbed down the steps and ran to the door.

She opened it very cautiously in case anyone was coming towards the Library.

To her relief, there was no-one in sight.

There was, she had noticed when going to the Library, a secondary staircase.

She knew it would take her up to the first floor.

She found it and climbed up the stairs quickly.

She guessed, when she reached the first floor, that the Highwaymen were sleeping there.

As she went up another staircase to the second floor, she thought it was really quite clever of them to seize such a remarkable opportunity as presented itself in the Marquis's absence.

She was quite certain the local people would never suspect that a Highwayman would dare to billet himself in a house as fine as Melverley.

They would have too much respect for the Marquis, even in his absence, to go looking round uninvited.

In fact, while she had thought it a good place to hide, so had the Highwaymen.

She wondered what the Marquis would say if he became aware of what was going on.

Nanny was waiting for her, and said as she entered the Nursery:

"You're late. I was beginning to worry as to what had happened to you."

"I had a lovely ride on *Apollo*," Imilda answered, "and I also rode another horse, a young one which is not getting enough exercise."

"That must have pleased old Abbot," Nanny said. "He fair breaks his heart over those horses."

"Yes, he was very pleased," Imilda said, "and I promised I would ride another of the horses tomorrow."

"Where did you get those books?" Nanny asked suddenly in a sharp voice.

"I went to the Library before I came up here," Imilda replied. "I cannot live without books to read."

"You should not have done that," Nanny scolded her. "I'll get you any books you want, but keep away from the Library."

Imilda thought of telling her that she now knew the reason why, but decided it would be a mistake.

She had a great deal more to find out.

If it was suspected that she was spying, perhaps even Nanny would side with the others to turn her out of Melverley.

"I am sorry," she said aloud, "if I have done anything wrong. When I have read these books, I will ask you where I can find some others."

"You tell me what you want," Nanny said, "and I'll get them for you. It's just that Mrs. Gibbons does not like people walking about in the State Rooms which are, of course, kept for His Lordship."

As Nanny spoke, she looked guilty.

Imilda knew that it went against the grain for her to lie, just as she had brought up the children she looked after never to tell a fib.

At the same time, Imilda was very eager to learn more.

She realised that now it was getting late in the afternoon.

The rest of the Highwaymen would be coming back from their business of robbing travellers and anyone else they encountered.

She was therefore expected to stay in the Nursery and not go anywhere else.

"As long as I can read, I shall be perfectly happy," she told herself.

At the same time, she was intensely curious.

She wanted to learn more about the men who had been clever enough to take over this house and make it their headquarters.

She was quite certain they had dispensed with their own horses.

They would not have been as well-bred as the Marquis's which they undoubtedly were now using.

They also slept in the Marquis's comfortable beds and their food was cooked in his Kitchen.

She could understand the younger servants had been intimidated into leaving.

Or they had run away because they had no wish to be involved.

The Highwaymen were therefore left with just a skeleton staff of the old servants who had nowhere else to go and had a horror of ending up in the Work-house.

There were a thousand questions Imilda wanted to ask Nanny, but she knew it would only agitate her.

Moreover, she must not say or do anything that would end in her being compelled to leave Melverley.

She was very fortunate to be hiding successfully where she was so comfortable.

Besides, being with Nanny she felt protected.

'It would be very silly of me to make a fuss," she thought. 'I shall just pretend my eyes are shut and that I neither see nor hear anything unusual.'

At the same time, she knew that the Marquis would have to deal with this sooner or later.

She wondered how he would manage it.

Soon she found that she could not help longing to see what they had stolen from their unhappy victims.

'I must see it! I must!' Imilda thought.

There was a secret passage in their house at home, and she had played in it as a child.

It was only a very short one, because when her Grandfather added the new wing, they blocked off most of it.

She was quite certain that the secret passage in Melverley would be a very important one.

It would have been used in the reign of Elizabeth to hide the Catholics whom she persecuted in the same way that her sister Mary had persecuted the Protestants.

The Royalists would have used it when Oliver Cromwell and his Roundheads were harrying them.

Those who could not flee, as the future King Charles II had done, to France, could keep alive only by hiding in the secret passage and sleeping in what had been the Priest's room.

A maid Imilda had not seen before, who was also elderly, came up to take away the supper dishes.

Imilda went to her own room.

The door of the Nursery was open, and they did not realise she could hear what they said.

"Is everything all right downstairs?" Nanny asked in a voice a little above a whisper.

"They've had a good day and be drinking themselves silly," the maid replied.

"Then they're all there?" Nanny asked.

"All eight o' them," the maid answered, "and Mrs. Gibbons be giggling like a school-girl. I don't know what m' Mother would say to the likes of her, that I don't."

"Be careful," Nanny said warningly, "or she'll push you out."

"Her finds me too useful for that," the maid answered. "There's too much work for me as it is, looking after eight men, as I tells her."

Nanny sighed.

"I know you do your best, Edie," she said, "but things aren't what they ought to be."

"You can say that again!" Edie replied.

She picked up the tray which was now laden with plates and bowls and walked towards the door.

"You can be sure them lot'll be drinking until they're under the table," she said. "They've had a haul and the way they talks they might have got th' Crown Jewels."

She gave a laugh at her own joke and went out into the passage.

Nanny shut the door after her.

Imilda knew she had heard what she wanted to know.

She waited until Nanny had gone to bed and everything was quiet.

Then she crept out of her Bedroom.

She went downstairs bare-footed so that she did not make a sound on the thick carpet.

There was, of course, no night-footman in the hall as there would have been if the Marquis had been in residence.

There were a few lights burning in the passages, so it was not difficult for Imilda to find her way to the Library.

It was in darkness, but she took a candle from one of the sconces outside.

Carrying it carefully, she found her way to the mantelpiece.

The panel through which Bill and the other man had disappeared was beside it.

Because she knew how to open the secret panel at home, it was not difficult for her to find a catch in the decorative carving that was very much the same.

When she pressed it, the panel opened slowly and she stepped inside.

Holding the lighted candle in her hand, she saw on the floor there was a candle-lantern.

It was obviously kept there for anyone who wished to use the secret passage.

She lit the candle in it and, to avoid arousing suspicion, she replaced the lighted candle in the sconce outside the Library.

Then, very slowly and feeling extremely excited, she walked down the narrow passage.

It was made so ingeniously that there was fresh air coming in from outside.

But she could not see how or where it actually came from.

She did not have to walk very far before she came to what she knew was the Priest's room.

It was where he said Mass for Catholics in secret.

She lifted the lantern to see what was on the floor, and gave a gasp.

The Highwaymen's spoil was very impressive.

They had not bothered to pack up what they had stolen.

They had just put it down on the floor in heaps.

There was a large pile of jewellery: diamond and emerald necklaces, brooches, ear-rings and finger-rings, all jumbled together.

They glittered in the light of the lantern.

There was another heap of fur coats, coats trimmed or lined with fur, capes that must have been worn by women, and a number of fur rugs which were used in travelling-carriages.

There were many other miscellaneous articles, but Imilda did not stop to inspect them.

What she wanted was to see how far the passage extended and what could be seen from it.

Having walked some way further along, suddenly she was startled by the sound of voices and laughter.

It was then she realised she was nearing the Dining-Room.

Imilda put her lantern down on the floor in case it should shine into the room.

She soon found what they had in the secret passage at home—a peephole.

It was just large enough for her to see through it.

She thought it was part of the panelling which again was near the mantelpiece.

Now she could see clearly there were eight men seated round the Dining-Room table.

It was laden with bottles of wine which she suspected came from His Lordship's cellars.

She looked at the men one by one.

They were all rather coarse, common types, and she had the idea that two or three of them might have been soldiers.

They would have had no other way of earning a living.

The man sitting at the head of the table in a chair on which was carved the Melverley Coat of Arms was obviously the leader.

He looked rather better bred, and he spoke in a slightly more educated voice than the rest of them.

Looking at him, Imilda was quite certain it was he

who had banded the men together.

It was he who had led them into the dangerous trick of robbing the rich.

He was not drinking as much as the other men.

Watching his eyes flickering over them, Imilda knew that he was evil.

She felt he would stop at nothing to get his own way.

She gave a shiver, then closing the peephole, she picked up the lantern from the floor.

She did not turn back but walked a little further on.

She soon found, as she had anticipated, a ladder built into the wall which led up to another passage on the first floor.

She climbed up to the top of it.

It took her a little time to find the catch, and when she did so, a panel opened and she found herself in a Bedroom.

Because she had lived in a great house herself, she recognised that this was the Master Bedroom.

There was no doubt that the huge four-poster bed with the Melverley Coat of Arms embroidered at the back of it would be slept in by the Marquis if he were in residence.

To her surprise, she saw it was not being used at the moment, since the bed was not made up.

She thought that perhaps Mrs. Gibbons was being cautious just in case the Marquis arrived unexpectedly.

She stepped back through the panel and shut it.

Then, out of sheer curiosity, although she knew she should go back to bed, she walked further along the passage from the Master Bedroom.

She was not surprised to find there were peepholes into almost all the other Bedrooms on that landing.

She looked into one and realised that was where a Highwayman was sleeping.

She went on, moving slowly, just to see if there was a way of reaching the floor above.

Sure enough, at the very end of the passage there was another ladder built into the wall.

When she climbed up it, she knew that when she opened the door at the top she would be on her own landing.

She thought it had been most ingeniously thought out.

When the door, which again was a panel, opened, she found herself only a short distance from the Nursery.

She blew out the light in the lantern she had been carrying, put it down just inside the secret panel, and then shut it.

She told herself at the same time that, as soon as the Highwaymen left the next morning, she must put the lantern back where she had found it.

In the light from a sconce on the landing there was nothing to suggest that the closed panel concealed anything so important as a secret passage.

"I have found it!" Imilda told herself. "Who knows, I may, if things go wrong, find it very useful!"

She turned and hurried to her own Bedroom.

There was no sound from Nanny's room next door.

Imilda thought with relief there need be no explanations to make the following morning.

'Now,' she thought, 'I know exactly what is happening at Melverley. Although His Lordship may not be interested, it is very, very dangerous.'

chapter five

THE Marquis left Harsbourne House as early as possible and drove back to London in a towering rage.

He was furious that he had been tricked into marriage.

He had decided that he would not marry for many years yet, and then only to have an heir.

He was well aware of his own consequence, and that ambitious Mamas longed for their daughters to become the Marchioness of Melverley.

He therefore refused to take any notice of *débutantes*.

He concentrated on enjoying himself with the acclaimed Beauties of the *Beau Monde*.

Unlike most of his friends, he did not keep a Cyprian in a discreet little house in Chelsea or St. John's Wood.

He told himself that he disliked paying for favours received, not because he was mean, but because it somehow disgusted him.

He certainly did not need to pay for them.

Apart from being extremely handsome, he was amusing and excellent company.

As a matter of fact, he was generous with his money.

He sent the object of his affections a mass of flowers which would fill a conservatory.

He gave her any present she desired and which it was conventional for her to receive.

Fans, sunshades, gloves, and bottles of expensive French perfume were received almost daily by any Beauty in whom he was interested.

Unfortunately his *affaires-de-coeur* never lasted long.

The Marquis could not understand it himself.

Why did a woman whom he found one day utterly and irresistibly desirable suddenly irritate him?

Why did he find her conversation too boring to listen to any longer?

After the long years fighting with Wellington's Army and the time he spent with the Army of Occupation, the Marquis had found London extremely amusing.

It did not perturb him that there were bets in White's Club on how long his love affairs would last just as there were bets as to which of his horses would win at Newmarket.

"I have never worried about what people say behind my back," he said once, "as long as they are polite to my face."

This was a *bon mot* which was repeated a thousand times, but he really did mean it.

He had gone down to stay at Harsbourne House because he wanted to win the Earl's Steeplechase.

It was considered one of the most difficult and demanding in England.

He was at the time considering whether he should or should not have an affair with the *Contessa* di Torrio.

He had been warned it would be a mistake.

Yet the *Contessa* had made it very clear, the few times they had met in other people's houses, that she would welcome his advances.

She was a very beautiful Italian with dark hair and huge, dark eyes.

There was no doubt, the Marquis thought, that making love to her would be, if nothing else, a very fiery experience.

His close friends, however, had said to him:

"Don't be a fool, Vulcan! The *Conte*, who is a professional Diplomat, is wildly jealous, as he may well be, of his wife. To touch her would be putting your head into the lion's mouth."

To the Marquis this made the idea of approaching her even more interesting than before.

When he won the Steeplechase, he told himself his luck was in, but it might be a mistake to strain it too far.

There were a great number of other women who looked at him with an expression in their eyes which he knew only too well.

The message was unmistakable!

There was the wife of an elder Statesman who just before he left London invited him to dine with her.

"It is only a small party," she said, "as unfortunately my Husband will be away in the North."

This meant, as the Marquis was well aware, that when he arrived there would be only an elderly couple.

They would say immediately after the dinner was finished that they had to go home.

This would leave the Marquis alone with his hostess.

Convention had been observed. No-one could say there was anything wrong in dining so well chaperoned.

The Marquis had almost made up his mind that was where he would dine on the evening following his return to London.

Then when the Countess of Harsbourne accused him of compromising Lady Imilda by being found in her Bedroom, he realised he had been had for a mug.

So many of his friends had told him of the hazards they had encountered where young girls were concerned.

One of them, a young Earl, had been forced to marry an extremely plain girl.

Her Mother was clever enough to enlist the help of the Prince of Wales in persuading him that he had damaged her reputation.

He had unwittingly taken her into the garden after dinner one evening.

Someone had said there was going to be an eclipse of the moon, which he had thought would be interesting to watch.

Actually it had not happened.

What did happen was that the Prince of Wales told the Earl that the girl's Mother was deeply distressed.

The least he could do under the circumstances was to ask her to marry him.

The Marquis had been determined that this sort of thing should not happen to him.

He had, in fact, not given a thought to Lady Imilda until she spoke to him at dinner about the suffering in the country.

It was something he had never considered before.

Occasionally he had felt a little guilty at having decided never to set foot in Melverley Hall.

But he told himself that he was entirely justified in that decision and no-one would make him change it.

The Hall typified everything that had made his life after his Mother's death a misery beyond words.

When his Father died and he became his own Master, he realised he never need speak to his Stepmother again.

He had given orders for her to leave the house and had made provision for her.

But even after she died two years before, he felt Melverley was still tainted by her cruelty and that he would never be able to enter his home without feeling she was still there scowling at him.

His Secretary and Manager, Mr. Richardson, sent him a monthly account of the expenses.

He did not even bother to read it.

He merely turned it over to his Secretary in London and told him to deal with it.

When he wanted to go to the country, he went to Newmarket.

He had fifteen excellent race-horses there and had every intention of building up his Stable further.

He bought a house which fortunately came on the market at exactly the right moment on the death of a Peer who had inhabited it for the last twenty years.

It was near the race-course and stood in five hundred acres of good agricultural land.

The Marquis planned to develop much of it as a Partridge Shoot.

When people asked what he was doing about Melverley and if the gardens were as beautiful as they had always been, he answered them evasively.

"I do not know and I do not care," he told himself.

"Let the house fall down brick by brick. I will not raise a finger to save it."

He drove back to London in his travelling-chaise drawn by four well-matched horses he had bought two months ago at Tattersall's.

He told himself furiously that he did not want a wife spoiling the parties he had been giving at New-market.

Nor did he want a wife interfering with his arrangements at Melverley House in Park Lane.

He could not even remember exactly what Lady Imilda looked like.

He vaguely thought she was not unprepossessing.

But she was just another *débutante* who in their white dresses kept in the background at the parties he frequented.

"How could I be caught in a trap in this idiotic manner?" he raged.

He knew only too well it was a deliberate trap from which he could not escape without causing a scandal.

He was well aware it had all been contrived by the Countess of Harsbourne.

From the moment he arrived he had thought she was a tiresome woman.

The way she monopolised him the first night at dinner, and the manner in which she tried to flirt with him, reminded him of his Stepmother.

Anyway, the Countess was too old to be of any interest to him and he had always been very fond of the Earl.

He would have been ashamed to intrude into his private life when he had shown him nothing but kindness.

Although people would not have believed it, the Marquis had his own set of rules as to how a Gentleman should behave, and he stuck to them.

In his opinion, men should look after their wives properly, not, as so many men did, spend their time gambling at the Club or shooting and fishing in the country.

In that way they opened the door to intruders like himself.

They had no right to complain if anything happened in their absence.

It had never crossed his mind for a moment that staying at Harsbourne House was likely to prove dangerous, except, of course, in relation to the Steeplechase.

Now he was returning to London in a fury, engaged to a girl in whom he had not the slightest interest.

"Why was I such a fool to go into her room when she screamed?" he asked himself.

He wondered if the girl herself was privy to the plot to trap him.

When he thought it over, he decided it was unlikely.

She had seemed very positive in declaring there was a rat in her room.

Also, he remembered that when he had gone to her assistance she was undoubtedly trembling.

There was, too, a note of horror in her voice which he did not think any actress, however brilliant, would be able to simulate.

'No,' he thought, 'it is that ghastly Countess who worked it all out.'

He had been told she was a Social climber.

He remembered now that people had been very surprised when the Earl who was known to be so happy with his first wife, married again.

'She caught him, as she has caught me,' the Marquis decided, and felt the anger rising again inside him.

Those who knew him well were aware that when he was angry, he appeared almost to freeze into himself.

If, in the Army, he reprimanded a man who had done something wrong, he spoke slowly and clearly, without raising his voice.

Yet the man would go pale and tremble as if the Marquis had actually threatened him with violence.

When he arrived in London, his staff, who admired him greatly for his brilliance in the war, realised apprehensively that he was in a strange mood.

Hardly saying a word, the Marquis went straight to his Study.

This was a large and comfortable room overlooking the garden at the back of the house.

His Secretary had arranged on the writing-desk the letters which had been delivered since the Marquis left London.

On one side were the letters which had been opened and were waiting for his inspection.

On the other side were the letters his Secretary left unopened because he recognised the hand-writing.

There were quite a number of these letters.

The Marquis looked through them a little disdainfully.

There were two from a Beauty who had already asked him to dine.

Then there was one in a pale blue envelope.

His name was written in extremely elegant hand-writing, but it did not look entirely English.

For the first time, the Marquis's face relaxed a little.

There was just a faint twist to his lips which had not been there before.

The letter was from the *Contessa* di Torrio, thanking him for the flowers he had sent her.

She said that she hoped to see him soon.

She wrote:

"My Husband has been recalled to Italy for a consultation. At the moment I am finding London very lonely."

The Marquis smiled as he put the letter back into the envelope. He knew where he would spend the evening!

At least that was what he hoped.

He had not expected to return to London so early in the day, and had thought if he dined with anyone, it would be the following evening.

Now he told himself there was no point in waiting.

He despatched a quickly scribbled note to the *Contessa* saying that, if it was convenient, he would call on her at seven-thirty that evening.

He gave the note to his Secretary.

He told him to send a groom with the letter to the *Contessa* and to wait for an answer.

He was sure it was extremely unlikely to be anything but in the affirmative.

The *Contessa*'s house, which was south of Hyde Park, was in its way like every other house in the Crescent.

The *Contessa* was clever enough to give it an individual touch which was as alluring and unusual as herself.

Diplomats from the different independent Kingdoms, Duchies, and States which were restored in Italy when the war with Napoleon ended had come to London.

They had suffered as many other Countries in Europe had suffered under the hard heel of the Emperor.

The British, led by the Prince Regent, were noted for being friendly and pleasant to those who had been adversaries.

The *Contessa* and the other Italians with her were astonished to find the Social doors of fashionable London were open to them.

They were treated as if during the years of war they had been friends and only involuntary enemies.

Because the *Contessa* was so beautiful, London acclaimed her.

The fashionable young men from White's paid her fulsome compliments which she found enchanting.

However, like so many other women, she had found it impossible to ignore the attractiveness of the Marquis.

That there were a number of women ready to warn her of his reputation merely made him more fascinating.

When she received his note to say he was coming to dinner, her household was galvanized into action.

Flowers were hurriedly bought from the nearest shops.

The Chef was told to prepare his best dishes.

The *Contessa* herself spent two hours concentrating on her face and her clothes before she went down to the Drawing-Room to wait for the Marquis's arrival.

He swept into the room looking even more handsome and more raffish than she remembered.

When she held out her hand he raised it to his lips and actually kissed it.

"You are beautiful," he said, "more beautiful than anyone I have ever seen!"

That was the beginning of a wildly passionate affair

in which the flames, the Marquis felt, rose higher and higher every night.

It was not interrupted by the publication in the *London Gazette* of his engagement to Lady Imilda Bourne.

This, of course, caused consternation from St. James's throughout Mayfair.

Most people found it difficult to believe it was actually true.

Letters poured into Melverley House in Park Lane.

They asked how it had happened. When was he to be married? When could they give a party for Lady Imilda and himself?

The Marquis ignored them all.

He found the *Contessa* made him forget what lay ahead, and concentrated only on her.

They were careful not to be seen together in public.

They were, however, together in private every hour of the day that it was possible.

Either the Marquis came to her house or she came to Park Lane.

The piles of invitations grew and grew, but the Marquis did not even bother to read them.

The only thing that slightly surprised him was that the Earl did not come with his family to London.

This meant, the Marquis thought thankfully, that he would not yet have to face that embarrassing moment of meeting the girl to whom he was officially but involuntarily engaged.

He assumed she was elated by the idea, but to him it was a fate worse than death.

"What shall we talk about?" he asked himself. "What shall we do? What the hell have I got in common with a young girl who has seen nothing of the world and has been closely chaperoned from the time she wakes up until the time she goes to bed?"

He thought of the women he had enjoyed in Paris before they bored him.

He thought of the fun he had found in London.

When he started to count his conquests, he was slightly ashamed.

Whatever it was, marriage with an inexperienced country-bred young woman would bore him to distraction.

He did not want to think. He did not want to plan. He did not even want to remember he was to be married.

So he concentrated on the *Contessa*.

"No-one," she whispered, "has ever had a more wonderful, a more marvellous or more ardent lover."

The Marquis thought he could say the same to her.

It was easy to kiss her and feel the fire burning on their lips.

Then, inevitably, they went too far.

The Marquis could never decide afterwards the truth of what happened.

Did the *Contessa* forget that her Husband was returning, or did he deliberately plan to surprise her?

It was after dawn, and the Marquis was, in fact, just leaving.

He had dressed himself quickly and efficiently.

The years of war had taught him that.

He turned from the mirror on the mantelpiece, having tied his cravat precisely, leaving the points of his collar high above his jawbone.

It was then the door opened and the *Conte* walked in.

The *Contessa* was lying naked in bed and gave a scream of horror.

The *Conte* stood in the doorway for the moment, seemingly frozen into immobility.

Then, as the Marquis turned round, he said, almost spitting the words at him:

"I will kill you for this."

The Marquis hesitated.

He tried to think of some explanation or excuse he could make for being in the *Contessa*'s bedroom.

But as he saw the hatred and fury on the Italian's face, he merely replied:

"In Green Park tomorrow evening at the usual hour."

Then with a dignity which was most commendable, he bowed to the *Contessa* and walked past the *Conte* and down the stairs without looking back.

As he drove home in the carriage which was waiting for him outside, he told himself he had made a hideous error.

The Prince Regent had more or less banned duels, particularly those which involved foreigners.

They were not to take place because they made a great deal of trouble not only for the Secretary of State for Foreign Affairs but also for the Prime Minister.

There was, however, as the Marquis knew, nothing he could do about it.

He could only hope that the *Conte* was not as skilled a duellist as he was reputed to be.

The two friends, however, whom he had asked to be his Seconds, made it quite clear that he had a very dangerous opponent.

"I have heard he has won duel after duel in Italy," one of them said. "There was a terrible scandal in Paris when he wounded one of Napoleon's most distinguished Statesmen."

"You are making me depressed, Charlie," the Marquis answered.

"You have reason to be," Charlie replied. "These

Italians are very quick off the mark, and I have a suspicion that he turns before the count of ten."

"Surely you cannot say that," the Marquis protested.

"Well, it is only a whisper, of course," Charlie went on, "but I do beg of you, Vulcan, to be on your guard. We have no wish to lose you."

"I have no wish to lose myself," the Marquis replied.

He had fought two duels in the past, one when he was very young, and one a year earlier.

On each occasion, quite undeservedly he was the winner, while the affronted Husband carried his arm in a sling for two months.

The men he had fought then had not been Italian.

Nor had they had the reputation with a duelling pistol which the *Conte* had.

The next day, because he obviously could not be with the *Contessa*, the Marquis opened some of his letters.

He found one from the Earl saying he was sorry he had not been able to come to London as he had intended.

His daughter, Imilda, was suffering from Spring fever, and they had had to stay in the country.

It was quite a short letter, and the Marquis tossed it on one side as unimportant.

He thought it was a good thing that the Earl had not come to London.

Otherwise he would have had to go to a number of parties to which he and his *fiancée* had been invited.

He could imagine nothing more boring and nothing that would make him more angry.

How could he pretend he was marrying for love?

He had been foolish enough to be caught in a trap

like any greenhorn with no experience of the Social World.

Once again he was hating the Countess, but knew, at the same time, it was useless.

He was a lamb being taken to the slaughter and there was nothing he could do about it.

He got bored with the pile of letters and threw the last dozen to one side.

He told himself he would go to the House of Lords.

He did not admit to himself why he made this decision.

Actually it was because he did not want to go to his Club.

If he did, he would have to answer uncomfortable questions about his engagement, or even more uncomfortable ones about the duel.

He had sworn his two Seconds to silence, but could not help feeling that somehow it would leak out.

The Clubs would be talking, just as the Drawing-Rooms would be whispering.

In the House of Lords there were the usual number of sleepy old Peers.

To his surprise, he was greeted by quite a number of them.

"It is nice to see you here," they said, "and congratulations on your Award. I have not seen you since you came home, or I would have spoken to you about it before."

An hour later, to the Marquis's surprise, he found himself rising to his feet in the Chamber.

He asked the Lords if anything had been done for the 30,000 men from the Army of Occupation with whom he had returned to England last year.

"Has any help been given them," he enquired, "to

find employment after serving their country so gallantly?"

He urged that preparation should be made now for when the remainder returned eventually.

He had heard very disturbing reports concerning the treatment of the men who had already been disbanded from the Army, especially those who had been wounded.

He could not believe that this was the way the country wished to thank those who had fought so bravely against Napoleon.

If, as he suspected, nothing was being done, then surely it was Their Lordships' duty to see that steps were taken immediately to ensure the future of the remaining 120,000 troops who would return at the beginning of the following year.

After the Marquis had sat down, quite a number of the older members came up to congratulate him.

"A very good speech, my boy," they said. "We shall hope to hear from you again. That is exactly the sort of thing men of your age should be thinking about and saying. We need waking up!"

The Marquis went back to Melverley House feeling gratified and slightly happier.

However, the hours passed slowly.

As he and his Seconds ate and drank in the vast Dining-Room, he felt as if a cloud of darkness were descending on him.

"Cheer up, Vulcan," Charlie said. "You have been lucky before, and I am sure you will be lucky again."

The Marquis was thinking that if only the *Conte* had come a quarter of an hour later, he would have left the house.

And if the *Contessa* had not been so foolish, she would have known the date of her Husband's return.

He had to admit he himself had let things slide.

He had not been on his guard as he would have been in war-time.

His friends were getting out the duelling pistols, inspecting and loading them.

When they drove towards Green Park, the Marquis said:

"This is the last time I will ever fight a duel."

Then he saw the expression on the faces of his friends.

Had he been prophetic and proclaimed his own death?

It was a warm night with no wind, and the moon was high over Green Park.

The Marquis sent his Seconds ahead.

While they were talking to the Referee, an elderly man, they saw the *Conte* arrive.

He had two Italians with him, and the Marquis thought they looked grim and rather unpleasant.

It might have been the colour of their skin, but they seemed to him to portend disaster.

"Now, be on your guard, Vulcan," his friend Charlie said. "Remember, he moves very quickly. Someone in the Club confirmed to me only today my warning that he turned too soon."

The two Duellers stood in front of the Referee, who repeated the familiar words of instruction in a bored voice.

Then they started to walk away from each other, the Marquis going East, the *Conte* West.

"Eight—nine—ten."

The *Conte* undoubtedly turned too quickly.

The Marquis, anticipating this, turned, but simultaneously moved sharply to his right.

The *Conte*'s shot rang out and was followed a second later by the Marquis's.

The *Conte* had been confident of winning.

As he turned fractionally early, he had shot at the same instant.

But, thanks to the Marquis's quick sideways movement, the *Conte*'s bullet missed while the Marquis's struck him in the chest and he collapsed onto the ground.

Finding it difficult to realise he was untouched, the Marquis walked towards his fallen opponent.

When he reached him, the Doctor who was in attendance was attempting to stop the flow of blood from the wound.

Charlie pulled the Marquis to one side.

"If he dies, Vulcan," he said, "it means you will have to spend at least a year abroad. If he lives, I will keep you informed."

He paused a moment and then went on:

"The best thing you can do now is to disappear. Go somewhere where the gossips cannot reach you and no-one can ask you awkward questions."

The Marquis put his hand on his friend's shoulder.

"Thank you, Charlie," he said, "I knew you would stand by me."

"Let me know where you are when you get there," Charlie said. "But hurry! All London will be talking about this before morning."

The Marquis drove back alone to Melverley House.

When he got there, he was let in by the footman on duty and walked straight up the stairs to his Bedroom.

As he expected, his Valet, Bates, who had been his Batman during the war, was waiting for him.

"How did yer get on, M'Lord?" Bates asked.

The Marquis told him what had happened.

"That's bad, real bad," Bates said. "Them foreigners be always the same, always have a trick up their sleeves. It's lucky yer're not lying down in his place."

The Marquis had thought this already and answered:

"I am still in a hell of a mess. I have got to go somewhere, Bates, where no-one will expect to find me, and I do not have to answer impertinent questions."

"I realises that, M'Lord," Bates said. "It means yer can't go to Newmarket."

"No, of course not," the Marquis agreed.

Bates thought for a moment, and then he said:

"Then why not Melverley, M'Lord? After all that's been said, no-one'll expect yer to be there."

"That is true," the Marquis murmured.

He walked across the room and drew back the curtain to look out at the moonlit garden.

He was thinking that his luck had deserted him and he had never been in such an uncomfortable position.

To go abroad was the last thing he wanted at the moment.

After spending so many years fighting Napoleon and then enduring the boredom of the Army of Occupation, he had longed to be in England.

At the same time, there was no place he wanted to go to less than Melverley, with its memories of crying himself to sleep, of being beaten whenever his Stepmother could contrive it, and hearing her voice in every room, jeering and jibing at him.

Then he told himself that everything had to be paid for and there is nothing free in this world.

He had enjoyed himself, and now there was the reckoning.

If it meant going to Melverley, it was a rough kind of justice.

"Very well, Bates," he said, "we will leave early in the morning for Melverley. You arrange it."

He turned back into the room as he spoke.

He thought that as far as he was concerned, the punishment exceeded the crime.

chapter six

IMILDA had been riding the second young horse which she had promised to exercise.

By this time she had both of them well under control and they enjoyed their ride as much as she did.

She always felt, however, a little guilty if she did not take *Apollo* first.

She therefore had taken *Apollo* out for two hours, immediately after an early breakfast.

She felt he enjoyed the new country they rode over as much as she did.

As she grew more familiar with the Marquis's Estate, she admitted that in some places it was even more beautiful than where she rode at home.

She was, however, always worried that something would happen to bring the Marquis to Melverley, which would, of course, compel her to leave and go somewhere else.

But she could not imagine where.

She put the young horse, who was called *Rufus*, into his Stable.

As old Abbot started to unsaddle him, she walked away towards the house.

She was late for luncheon, but she felt sure Nanny would understand.

She went in as usual through the back-door.

Then, as she walked past the larders, she heard a tremendous commotion in the Kitchen.

She could not imagine what was going on.

A moment later she saw the Kitchen-door was open and there were a number of people there all shouting at once.

She paused and heard Mrs. Gibbons scream:

"We will have to stop him, we will have to stop him!"

Then Hutton, the Butler, said a little less loudly:

"You know that's impossible. If 'e wants to come 'ome, who's to stop 'im?"

"What has happened? What is wrong?" Imilda asked.

She knew the answer almost before she heard it.

"We've had a message from 'Is Lordship. 'E be on 'is way 'ere," Hutton replied.

Imilda drew in her breath.

This might affect the household, but it even more certainly affected her.

"What time is he arriving?" she asked in a voice which did not sound like her own.

The servants were all talking at once.

They were making such a noise that Hutton had to come closer so that she could hear what he was saying.

"His Lordship sent a groom early this morning to tell us he was on his way. I reckons if he leaves after breakfast, say ten o'clock, he should be here within an hour or two. That's if he stops for luncheon on the way."

Hutton was obviously working it out slowly in his own mind, but Imilda understood.

She did not wait for him to say any more, but hurried up the side staircase to Nanny.

"You're late!" Nanny said as Imilda came into the Nursery. "If your luncheon's cold, it is your own fault."

"I know that," Imilda said, "but there is a terrible commotion going on downstairs."

Nanny stiffened.

"What has happened?" she asked.

"His Lordship is on his way here."

She thought Nanny would be delighted at the news.

She talked so often of how she longed to see "Master Vulcan," as she called him.

Sometimes, when she was more sentimental and talking of him as a child, she would refer to him as "my baby."

But she said in a very different tone from what Imilda expected:

"He must not come here, it'd be a great mistake."

"I know what is worrying you," Imilda said quietly, "but I imagine someone could send them away as soon as they return to the house this evening."

Nanny looked at her.

"So you know what I'm talking about?"

Imilda nodded.

"I saw two of them by mistake," she said, "and after that I was aware why eight horses were taken out of the Stables every morning."

"What'll His Lordship say to that, I'd like to

115

know?'' Nanny asked. "They be his horses and they've no right to them, that they haven't.''

"I can understand it was a temptation they could not resist,'' Imilda said. "But what are you going to tell His Lordship when he arrives?''

"I'm not going to tell him anything,'' Nanny said. "It's not my business. I didn't ask them here. It's that Mrs. Gibbons carrying on disgraceful with the men that brought them in the first place.''

It was what Imilda had suspected, but that was not the problem at the moment.

What really mattered was how the Marquis was going to deal with the Highwaymen and the Highwaymen with him.

Imilda sat down and ate her luncheon which, as Nanny said, had grown cold.

She was, however, not taking much notice of what she was eating.

She was worrying about herself and how she could hide from the Marquis.

'Perhaps,' she thought, 'he is coming only for a short visit just to see how things are here. In which case there is no reason why he would see me or have any idea I am staying here.'

She waited until she had finished luncheon and then said to Nanny:

"For reasons I do not want to explain, I have no wish to see the Marquis or to speak to him.''

Nanny looked surprised.

"But he sent you here to look after the Herb Garden,'' she said. "He'll surely want to hear how you're doing.''

"I doubt if he will remember,'' Imilda answered. "If he does, he will not be interested in hearing about me. So please, Nanny, do not mention my name, and when he comes up to see you, I will hide."

Nanny put her hands up to her forehead.

"I don't know what's a-going on," she said, "that I don't. I think if you ask me, things'll blow up in this place and not before time."

"I agree with you," Imilda said, "but, please, Nanny, remember not to mention my name or remind the Marquis I am here."

She went into the Bedroom as she spoke so that she would not hear Nanny's answer.

She could only pray that no-one would bother about her.

There would be so many other things to talk about, and she hoped the Marquis would leave without having any idea she was staying in his house.

Because she did not want to go anywhere where she might be seen, she stayed in the Nursery during the afternoon.

Nanny went downstairs to find out what was happening.

When she came back to the Nursery, Imilda asked:

"What are they doing?"

"A lot of things as ought to have been done before," Nanny said sharply. "They're cleaning and polishing, and hoping His Lordship'll not ask too many questions."

"You mean they are trying to conceal the fact that the Highwaymen have been living here."

"They *are* living here," Nanny replied. "Mrs. Gibbons says it is quite impossible to stop them arriving. They'll ride in from different directions and there's not enough servants in the house to intercept them all."

Imilda could understand this.

In fact, the only person unemployed at the moment was herself.

She looked at the clock.

It was later than she thought, and the Marquis had not arrived as Hutton expected soon after luncheon.

Time dragged on and there was still no sign of him.

Imilda began to hope that perhaps he had changed his mind and was not coming after all.

Because she was curious, she went down to the first floor.

She creeped along the corridor towards the Master Suite.

The doors were open and she thought they must have cleaned it and made up the bed.

She guessed, too, that the Highwaymen's things had all been taken out of the State Rooms adjoining it.

The Marquis would sleep alone in his glory.

He would have no idea who had occupied that part of the house the previous night and many before that.

Everything was very quiet and still.

Imilda moved a little further on so that she could look over the balustrade into the hall.

It looked much cleaner and well polished, certainly much smarter than she had ever seen it.

In fact, it looked so different that she thought if the Marquis did not come after all, it would really be rather disappointing.

"He must have changed his mind," she decided.

Looking at the Grandfather clock which someone had wound up for the first time since her arrival, she saw it was six o'clock.

This was the dangerous time, when the Highwaymen would be returning.

She supposed Mrs. Gibbons or one of the other servants would be waiting for them in the Stable-yard.

Even as she was wondering what might happen after that, she heard the sound of wheels.

A chaise was drawing up outside the front-door.

Hutton must have been on the alert although she had not seen him.

He came hurrying into the hall to open the door.

If the house was well polished, so was he.

As he opened the front-door, the Marquis came up the steps.

"Welcome home, M'Lord," Hutton said. "It's a joy to have Your Lordship with us again."

"Good evening, Hutton," the Marquis said, shaking hands with him. "I am later than I expected because I called to see my Mother's and Father's graves in the Church-yard, and the Vicar asked me in for tea."

Listening, Imilda wondered if the Vicar had said anything about the Highwaymen.

Then she realised it was most unlikely that he knew what was happening up at the Hall.

As she had learned from Nanny, Mrs. Gibbons had forbidden anyone to go into the village except herself.

Peeping round the corner, she had a quick glimpse of the Marquis.

He was looking, she thought, even more handsome than when she had seen him before.

He also appeared to be in a good humour.

If he had heard anything of what was happening in his home, he would certainly not be so agreeable to Hutton.

"There's Champagne ready for Yer Lordship in the Study," Hutton was saying. "And yer must forgive us if things be not exactly as yer expected, but we're very short-handed."

"Short-handed?" the Marquis replied. "Why is that?"

He was handing Hutton, as he spoke, his hat and gloves.

Hutton obviously had his answer ready.

"The young men, My Lord, went off to th' war like yerself, and th' young women found it dull here."

"I suppose I can understand that," the Marquis said.

He walked towards his Study with Hutton following him, and Imilda went back upstairs.

Nanny joined her and she learned they were struggling in the Kitchen to concoct a dinner which the Marquis would enjoy.

It would be ready soon after seven o'clock which was the time his Father always ate.

In that case, Imilda thought, it was unlikely the Marquis would inspect the Stables that evening.

"The person they're all worried about," Nanny said, "is His Lordship's Valet. Servants talk and they'll find it difficult to keep everything from him."

"What about his groom, or was he driving himself?" Imilda asked.

"I don't know," Nanny answered. "But I can't imagine His Lordship being driven by anybody."

There were so many questions to which Imilda wanted an answer.

But she told herself she would have to wait until the morning.

No-one came to clear the table in the Nursery.

Imilda and Nanny put the tray containing their plates and dishes outside in the passage.

"They'll be busy with His Lordship's dinner," Nanny said, "and I'm going to bed early. He'll not be asking to see me tonight, and I've got a headache with all this worry."

"I'm not surprised," Imilda said. "Let me make you a cup of tea while you go and get into bed."

She knew Nanny had been worrying all day about what would happen.

It had really been too much for her.

She made the tea and then told herself she was too curious to go to bed.

Suddenly an idea came.

She would wait a little longer, then go down the secret passage.

If the Highwaymen were in the house, she might be able to hear what they were intending to do.

She was sure that they would not leave without taking the pile of jewellery and everything else they had stolen with them.

This would mean they must wait until the Marquis was asleep before moving it from the Priest's room through the Library.

The more she thought of this, the more she was certain that was what would happen.

"I must hear where they are planning to go," she told herself, "and if they intend to return as soon as the Marquis leaves."

She wondered again how long he would stay.

It seemed very strange that he had come here so unexpectedly, unless there was a special reason for it.

Because she was so restless, she went in through the secret panel which was near the Nursery.

Reaching the bottom floor, she moved very silently along it, holding in her hand a lighted candle she had brought from her Bedroom, until she reached the peephole into the Study.

The Marquis was there, as she expected.

He was seated on the sofa and there was a newspaper beside him, but he was not reading it.

Instead, he was staring pensively ahead of him with what she thought were unseeing eyes.

It was obvious he was worrying about something.

She wished she could talk to him and find out why he had come home and what concerned him at this moment.

She was remembering how miserable he had been in Melverley as a boy, according to Nanny.

He had been treated cruelly by his Stepmother.

She felt that it must be something very urgent that had brought him home in this strange manner.

Unexpectedly, the Marquis yawned and got to his feet.

He pushed the newspaper aside and walked towards the door.

Then, remembering there were very few servants in the house, he blew out the candles one by one before he left the room.

'He is going to bed,' Imilda thought.

She picked up her candle and moved back the way she had come.

However, instead of going up the ladder to the next floor, she walked on.

She had no idea where the secret passage ended, but thought it might be somewhere near the Kitchen.

It did finally come to an end.

There was just a panel in front of her and she opened it very carefully.

She found that it came out, which she had not expected, in the passage from the back-door.

It was the one she had used herself when she came from the Stables.

Now she understood that this was a way of escape for anyone in hiding.

He could reach the Stables quickly and get away on a horse before being discovered.

It might have been used by Roundheads searching the house for its Royalist owner.

She stood at the open panel, listening.

Then she realised there were people talking in the Servants' Hall.

She put down her candle, pushed the panel to, and slipped across the passage into the larder.

She knew that the Servants' Hall was on the other side of it.

She thought she might be able to hear what was being said there.

She was not mistaken.

At the far end of the larder there was another door into the Hall.

It had obviously been used that evening.

A number of dirty plates had been put through the door onto a table near it in the larder.

As Imilda crept up to it, she could only hope there were no more to come.

When she reached the door, she found that luckily it was not completely closed.

It was pulled to, but she could see light at the edges of it and hear quite clearly what was being said inside the Servants' Hall.

She had not been mistaken in thinking that was where the Highwaymen would be.

She could hear their deep voices and Mrs. Gibbons's high one.

"Now what are you going to do?" Imilda heard her ask. "Make your minds up, because you can't stay here."

"I don't know where we can go," a man answered.

She had heard his voice before, and Imilda thought it was Bill.

"There must be somewhere not too far away," Mrs. Gibbons said, "and you can come back as soon as he's gone."

"Perhaps us can sleep in one o' the barns for a night or two," one of the other men said.

"You'll have to leave the horses," Mrs. Gibbons went on. "You knows as well as I do His Lordship'll want to see 'em in their stalls tomorrow morning. It's just by luck that he hasn't gone up there tonight."

"How can we manage without our horses?" Bill asked. " 'Twas you as said get rid o' them as we 'ad when we came 'ere."

"They were all decrepit and not much use to any of you," Mrs. Gibbons said defensively.

"Us could do with 'em now," another man grumbled.

"I've got a better idea!"

The speaker, Imilda was sure, was the man whom she had seen sitting at the head of the Dining-Room table.

She had thought he was not only the ring-leader but was also evil.

"What is it, Rigg," Bill asked.

"We'll wait 'til he's asleep. Then we'll suffocate him in his bed, so there'll be no marks on him, and tip him into the lake."

There was a gasp from them all, but he went on:

"When they finds 'im, they'll think he was walking about and slipped in by mistake. No one'll suspect we've anything to do with it."

"It's certainly an idea," Mrs. Gibbons said. "Are you sure we won't be suspected?"

"Not if you keep your pretty lips closed," Rigg answered.

Imilda had heard all she wanted to hear.

Softly she moved across the tiled floor towards the other door.

She passed through the secret panel and, picking up her candle, she started to run.

She found the ladder which took her up to the first floor.

She moved along it until she reached the panel which opened into the Master Suite.

She looked through the peephole, thinking the Marquis might be undressing and Bates still with him.

It had, however, all taken much longer than she thought.

The room was in darkness.

There was just a faint light from the moon and stars showing on either side of the curtains.

She could just see that the Marquis was lying in the large four-poster.

Quickly she opened the panel door.

Holding the candle in her hand, she said:

"Wake up! My Lord! Wake up!"

She thought for a moment he had not heard her.

Then, as if he had not been asleep but merely lying in the darkness, he said:

"Who is it? Where are you?"

As he spoke, he raised himself in bed and could see Imilda standing by the mantelpiece.

"Please listen, My Lord," Imilda said. "Highwaymen have been using your house for lodging and they are coming up the stairs to strangle you and throw you into the lake. Come quickly into the secret passage where I am standing."

The Marquis stared at her.

"Is this some joke?" he asked.

"I assure you it is deadly serious," Imilda replied. "You must do what I tell you, or you will lose your life."

"I suppose I can have something to say in the matter," the Marquis said somewhat sarcastically.

"With eight to one against you?" Imilda asked scornfully. "Please do as I tell you. If I am mistaken and they do not come, then you can go back to bed and sleep peacefully."

There was an urgency in her voice that convinced the Marquis she was telling the truth.

Yet it seemed too extraordinary to be credible.

"Very well," he said. "I will do what you say. Is there time for me to dress?"

"It is not worth the risk," Imilda advised.

She was thinking it had taken her some time to reach him.

The Highwaymen could come up the main staircase far quicker than by her route.

"Hurry! Hurry!" she said frantically. "You will see your way if I stand inside the secret passage."

She stepped back into it as she spoke, having set her candle down on the floor.

The Marquis had a little light from it while she moved out of sight.

He got out of bed and picked up a long, dark robe which Bates had left for him over a chair.

He put on his bedroom slippers.

Telling himself that the whole thing must be part of this woman's imagination, he crossed the room.

Even as he did so, Imilda stopped him.

"Tidy the bed," she said in a whisper. "They will think you have gone out in the garden and look for you there."

The Marquis thought this sounded possible.

He pulled the sheets straight and plumped the pillow.

Once again he walked towards the panel.

As he reached it, he thought he heard footsteps in the passage outside the door.

Imilda picked up the candle, and as the Marquis joined her, she pushed the panel into place.

"You can watch through the peephole," she whispered.

"There is one I made myself to save my having to crouch."

The Marquis whispered his reply, but there was an amused note in his voice which had not been there before.

Imilda thought he was perhaps suspecting this was some kind of feminine trickery which he had not met before.

She said nothing but opened the peephole she had used previously.

She realized it was, in fact, very low for him.

He was standing beside her.

In case any light from the candle could show through, Imilda put it down again on the floor behind her.

Then, as she put her eye to the peephole, she saw the door of the Marquis's Bedroom being opened very slowly.

It was so silent that had he been in bed, he would have been unaware of it.

Two men came in followed by a third, who stood just inside the door as if keeping watch.

The other two crept towards the bed.

They were carrying something in their hands.

Imilda guessed it was cords to strangle him with,

or, more likely, some softer material which would not leave a mark.

The only light in the room came from the sconce in the passage outside the open door.

Then one of the men said in a whisper:

"There be no-one here."

The man at the door who Imilda now realised was Rigg, said:

"Are you sure?"

"The bed ain't been slept in," the third man announced. "He must have gone out into th' garden."

"Perhaps down to the lake? That'll make it easier for us," Rigg said. "Come on, boys, if we collect the others, there'll be no chance of his getting away."

The way he spoke made Imilda shiver.

Not only was there ruthlessness in his voice, but she could tell he was enjoying the idea of murdering the Marquis.

They went out of the room, closing the door behind them.

It was only then that Imilda realised that as they watched, she had, without thinking, put out her hand towards the Marquis.

He had taken it into his.

Because he knew she was frightened, his fingers had tightened to reassure her.

Without taking her hand away, she said:

"Now you understand, I was right."

"I can only thank you for saving me," the Marquis said quietly. "What do we do now?"

"First you must have some clothes," Imilda answered, "then I thought, but I may be wrong, that you should get the help of the Army."

She picked up the candle as she spoke, then realised the Marquis was staring at her.

After a moment he said:

"Of course, that is what I should do."

"You will want your riding-clothes," Imilda said, "but you must stay here in the passage in case they come back."

"What if they find you there?" the Marquis enquired.

"I will say I am a servant and have come to tidy the room," Imilda said quickly. "But actually I think we are quite safe."

She put the candle into the Marquis's hand as she spoke and opened the panel door.

Then, as she walked towards the wardrobe, she realised he had followed her.

"I told you to stay in the secret passage," she said.

"If you are brave," he answered, "I have to be brave too."

"Then hurry!" Imilda begged.

The Marquis opened the wardrobe where Bates had arranged the clothes they had brought from London.

He took out all he wanted, including his riding-boots.

Then he walked towards the panel and Imilda followed him.

Everything was very quiet, but she was still frightened.

Only when they were inside the secret passage and the panel was closed could she breathe again.

"Where do we go from here?" the Marquis asked.

"I think the safest place, where they are unlikely to look, is with Nanny," Imilda answered.

"Nanny!" the Marquis exclaimed. "I had forgotten she would be here."

"She has not forgotten you," Imilda answered.

She did not say any more, but started down the passage.

She went slowly, because she knew the Marquis would find it difficult carrying both his clothes and his boots.

When they reached the ladder up to the second floor, Imilda said:

"I will go up first. Then if you hand me your boots, I will push them through into the passage. You will find it easier to climb without them."

The Marquis gave a little laugh, as if he were amused, but did not say anything.

He merely did as he was told.

Imilda opened the door into the Nursery.

As she had expected, Nanny had gone to bed and it was in darkness.

She lit the candles, then went into Nanny's bedroom.

"Nanny!" she said softly.

Nanny woke immediately.

"What is it? What is wrong?" she asked.

"You have a visitor I know you will want to see," Imilda replied. "He is in the Nursery."

Nanny gave a little cry.

"He is safe, he is not in trouble?"

"Because I want him to be safe, I have brought him to you," Imilda said. "Now, put on your dressing-gown, Nanny, and come and join us."

She left Nanny getting out of bed and went into the Nursery.

The Marquis had put his clothes down on a chair and was sitting on another one.

This was the moment Imilda thought that he might recognise her.

As she came towards him, she thought he was looking at her curiously, but not as if he had ever seen her before.

"What can I say to you?" he asked as she reached him. "It is difficult to express what I feel in words."

"Then do not try," Imilda said. "You have no idea what a commotion you have caused by coming home so unexpectedly."

"Why did you not come and tell me as soon as I arrived, what is happening here at Melverley?"

"I am a newcomer myself," Imilda answered. "I was warned not to leave the Nursery after six o'clock at night, and discovered only by chance that is when the eight Highwaymen return with the booty they have stolen during the day."

She paused a moment and then went on:

"They eat and sleep in great comfort in a house where no-one would dream of looking for them."

"What has happened to Mr. Richardson?" the Marquis asked.

"I was told he is ill," Imilda answered. "But if he is just frightened, it is understandable."

"You say there are eight of these men?"

"Yes, eight, and they are riding your horses."

The Marquis's lips tightened for a moment, and then he said:

"I never thought of anything like this happening."

Imilda made no comment, and after a moment he went on:

"But I suppose I should have come back before now to see for myself."

"One can hardly blame the Highwaymen," Imilda said, "for taking advantage of what to them was a heaven-sent opportunity."

The Marquis laughed.

"I suppose I should also forgive them for wanting to kill me."

"Which they still intend to do," Imilda reminded him.

He frowned.

"You said I should get the Army to help. How do you suggest I do that?"

"It is not really very difficult. They are on manoeuvres only about three miles from here."

"I shall certainly ask their assistance," the Marquis answered. "The difficulty, of course, is how to get out of the house without the Highwaymen seeing me and stopping me."

"I have already thought of that," Imilda replied.

He looked at her, and once again he was smiling.

"I cannot believe," he said, "that you are real. You are obviously my Guardian Angel disguising herself as a human being, or perhaps you are a goddess who has come down from Olympus to inspire a mere mortal."

Imilda laughed.

"I wish I were either of such beings. Now I will tell you what I think we can do."

"I am listening," the Marquis said.

At that moment Nanny came into the room.

She had tidied her hair and arranged it in the same way she wore it in the daytime.

Her dressing-gown of pink flannel trimmed with crocheted lace was buttoned neatly at her neck.

Imilda liked the way the Marquis jumped to his feet.

"Nanny!" he exclaimed.

Putting his arms round her, he hugged her and kissed her on both cheeks.

"I have missed you," he said.

"As I've missed my boy," Nanny answered.

She was smiling, but at the same time she was very near to tears.

"Now, sit down, Nanny," Imilda said. "We have to plan how His Lordship can get away from the Highwaymen. They are trying to murder him."

Nanny gave a cry of horror.

"I thought those devils would think of something like that," she said. "Oh! Master Vulcan, you've no idea what we've been through here with them taking over the house, and that Mrs. Gibbons encouraging their wicked ways."

"I will cope with everything, Nanny," the Marquis promised. "But first, as this kind young lady has been telling me, I must get the help of the Army."

"I guessed Miss Graham would warn you they are bad men," Nanny said.

"They planned to suffocate him in his bed," Imilda told her, "and put his body in the lake so that people would think he had drowned by accident."

Nanny gave a cry of horror.

"They are wicked, real wicked! I don't know what your Father'd say to their being here in your own home."

"It is something that will never happen again, Nanny, I promise you," the Marquis said. "It is my fault this has happened, because I have stayed away too long."

"Far, far too long," Nanny answered. "I've been praying every night for you to come back."

"Your prayers are answered," the Marquis said as he smiled, "and now I have to save not only myself but you and Miss Graham from being molested by such filth."

He looked towards Imilda and said:

"Now, tell me what I am to do."

"The Highwaymen have been riding your horses all day," Imilda said, "but *Apollo*, my horse, which I brought with me, has been out for only an hour or so. No-one will be surprised if very early in the morning I go to the Stables and ride him before I exercise the other horses which belong to you."

The Marquis was listening and she went on:

"What you have to do is to sleep for a little while and then slip out through the shrubbery and find your way, which should not be difficult for you, to the end of the paddock."

She drew in her breath, and said slowly:

"Be careful no-one sees you, although it is unlikely there will be anyone about. When I join you, you will take *Apollo* and ride to the Barracks. After that it is up to you what happens."

The Marquis looked at her, and then he said quietly:

"I promise if it is humanly possible, I will not let you down."

"That sounds to me a very sensible plan," Nanny said. "Now, Master Vulcan, you have a little sleep on the sofa. I'll make it comfortable for you and I'll call you whatever time Miss Graham says you should be slipping out of the house."

"I have found that there is a secret panel at the end of the passage, just before the Kitchen-door," Imilda said. "I expect you remember it."

"I think so," the Marquis answered, "but you had better come with me so that I do not make a mistake."

"I will do that," Imilda answered, "but you must not come to the Stables. Keep in the bushes and make your way to the far end of the paddock."

"Now I am completely at home," the Marquis said.

"I used to hide in the shrubbery, first from Nanny and then from my Tutor."

"A real mischief, you were!" Nanny exclaimed. "Time after time I've gone calling and calling you, and you up a tree laughing at me."

"I will not do it again," the Marquis answered.

Nanny hurried across the room to find blankets and a pillow for the large sofa.

Imilda thought perhaps she should offer him her bed.

Then she decided it might be somewhat embarrassing and he would be just as comfortable on the sofa.

Nanny insisted they all have a cup of tea, and after that they all went to bed.

"You promise you will call us," Imilda said a little nervously.

"I've never known m'clock fail yet," Nanny answered. "In any case, looking after babies I'm used to waking at any time it's necessary."

"And I learnt the same in the Army," the Marquis said, "so I think, Miss Graham, you will be the only one who might oversleep."

Imilda knew he was teasing her, and she replied:

"Just in case anything happens in the night or you hear anyone outside the door, which we will lock, please promise you will go and hide under Nanny's bed. They are not likely to look for you there."

"You do not think they'll be searching the whole house for you?" Nanny said in trembling voice.

"They will know he is somewhere and will be determined to find him," Imilda answered. "Therefore we have to be clever enough to outwit them."

Nanny picked up the cups from which they had been drinking and put them away in the sideboard.

Imilda knew she was thinking that if anyone came

in and saw there were three, they would be suspicious.

At the same time, it was difficult not to fear that anything might happen.

She was quite certain the Highwaymen would not give up the search easily.

She could imagine Rigg's frustration and anger when they kept reporting there was no sign of the Marquis.

Nanny locked the door into the Nursery and also the one into the Bathroom and her small Kitchen.

Her Bedroom door and Imilda's opened only into the Nursery itself.

"Now, rest while you've got the chance," she said to Imilda, "and that goes for you, Master Vulcan. You've driven down from London and had a shock at what is happening. It takes it out of you, whatever you may say."

"I am doing exactly what I am told, Nanny, and thank you both for looking after me," the Marquis said.

"You know what it means to me," Nanny said with a break in her voice. "We wants you here, we needs you here, and the truth is, we can't do without you."

"I realize that now," the Marquis said, "and if it is not too late, I will make amends."

He spoke seriously, and Imilda felt her heart leap.

The Marquis had come home and was staying home.

Now perhaps Melverley would look again as she wanted it to look.

Besides, she loved it!

Then, as the Marquis kissed Nanny goodnight, she went to her own Bedroom.

chapter seven

THE Marquis vanished into the bushes and Imilda walked on into the Stable-yard.

She could hear the eight horses moving in their Stable and went into the next.

Apollo was delighted to see her.

It was only just dawn, but there was enough light for her to find a man's saddle to put on *Apollo*.

Then she led him into the yard and rode into the paddock.

She was not surprised that there was no-one about, and old Abbot, who was slightly deaf, was not likely to hear her.

If he did, he would just think she had got up early.

What she had been afraid of was that the Highwaymen were still up and searching for the Marquis.

But as they came out of the panel and very quietly unbolted the back-door, Imilda had heard a sound of snoring from the Servants' Hall.

This meant at least some of the Highwaymen were sleeping there.

She was, however, certain that Mrs. Gibbons would have arranged for Rigg and herself to be in a comfortable bed upstairs.

Whatever was happening, the situation was very dangerous.

As she rode towards the end of the paddock, she was worrying about the Marquis.

When she reached the end of the field, she looked anxiously for him.

Then, as she drew *Apollo* to a standstill, he came out from the bushes.

"Was it all right?" he asked.

"No-one saw me leave," she answered.

She dismounted as she spoke and patted *Apollo* on his neck.

The Marquis took hold of the reins.

"You will be . . . careful," Imilda said, "and remember that each . . . one of them . . . has a loaded . . . pistol."

The Marquis smiled and replied:

"You take care of yourself and stay upstairs with Nanny until it is all over."

She thought he was being too casual about it, and looking up at him, she said again:

"Please . . . be . . . very . . . careful."

There was no answer.

But suddenly he bent forward and his lips were on hers.

It was such a surprise that Imilda stiffened.

Then, as the Marquis's kiss became more possessive, she felt something like a streak of lightning run through her.

Before she could move or even breathe, he had

sprung onto *Apollo*'s back and was riding away.

He did not look round, and she watched him until he was out of sight among the trees.

Then she put her hand up to her lips as if she could not believe it had happened.

It was the first time she had been kissed, and it was everything that she had believed a kiss should be.

Yet she had received it from the Marquis, the man from whom she was running away.

It was a few moments later before she realised she was standing in full view in the paddock.

If anyone saw her, they might be very suspicious.

She moved quickly until she was under the trees and then started to walk slowly back to the house.

It was a warm morning, and since she did not expect to see anyone except the Marquis, she was just wearing her riding-skirt, a thin muslin blouse, and no hat.

If on her return any Highwaymen did see her, she could say she was going to the Herb Garden, where they knew she worked.

But all she could really think of at the moment was the Marquis and how he had kissed her.

Then she told herself scornfully she was behaving like all the other women who ran after him because he was so handsome.

He had kissed her because he was grateful that she had brought him *Apollo*.

If she tried to read anything more into the gesture, she could be very foolish.

Of course, he kissed dozens of women because they attracted him.

The reason he had kissed her was simply that he was grateful.

"Be sensible," Imilda told herself, "and forget it. It

is something he will never think of again."

When she reached the house, she hesitated.

Should she go in through the front-door or the way she had left?

Because it was still very early, she thought it wiser to do the latter.

No-one saw her open the back-door or slip through the panel.

When she reached the Nursery, Nanny had a cup of tea waiting for her.

"He got away?" she asked as Imilda came in.

"No-one saw us," Imilda answered.

Nanny gave a deep sigh of relief,.

"Now we just have to hope," she said, "that he gets the soldiers here quick enough to catch them before they set off again, robbing decent folk who cannot protect themselves."

Imilda drank the tea Nanny had prepared for her.

She then went to her room and lay down on the bed.

She knew every minute that passed was going to seem like an hour before the Marquis came back with the soldiers.

She had no idea how they would round up the Highwaymen.

But she was sure that after his success in the war, he would work out a plan which would cause as little bloodshed as possible.

Then she wondered if, having cleared the intruders out of his house, he would return to London.

Some reason which she did not understand had brought him here.

What she wanted to know was if there was anything which would persuade him to stay.

She must have fallen asleep.

She had slept very little during the night, waking up several times to make sure it was not yet the dawn when Nanny was going to call them.

Now Nanny came into the Bedroom to say:

"I thinks things is happening."

Imilda jumped up off the bed.

"What do you mean? What have you heard?" she asked anxiously.

"It sounded like someone screaming," Nanny answered. "Oh! God help my baby if he's in trouble!"

Imilda made the same wish beneath her breath.

Then she opened the Nursery door and went out onto the landing to listen.

For a moment there seemed only silence, and she thought Nanny must have been mistaken.

Then she heard a shot followed by another!

Then there were several more which seemed to echo and re-echo up the stairs.

She was terrified.

She could only pray the Marquis had not underestimated the Highwaymen's determination to fight like cornered rats.

She was not to learn until later that his plan of capturing them had been brilliant.

He too had thought when they slipped out by the back-door that some of the Highwaymen were sleeping in the Servants' Hall.

When at the Barracks they knew who he was, the Officer in charge responded immediately to his request for help.

The soldiers the Marquis had brought with him left their horses, and the brake which had carried a number of them, in the wood at the back of the house.

They then approached through the shrubs and trees.

They moved silently, as they had been taught as part of their military training, until they reached the house.

The Marquis led them to the back-door and showed them the three windows of the Servants' Hall.

As it was so warm, they were all open at the bottom, as he had anticipated.

The soldiers crept up until they were beneath them.

Others led by the Marquis entered the Servants' Hall through the larder and by the door in the passage.

At the word of command, the soldiers pointed their guns at the five occupants of the room and ordered them to surrender.

They had no chance of doing anything else.

Although two men reached for their pistols, they realised it was impossible to use them.

The Marquis knew this left three Highwaymen unaccounted for.

He led six men who he thought looked more intelligent than the rest up the stairs to the first floor.

He guessed that Mrs. Gibbons and Rigg, the man Imilda had described to him, would be together.

They and the other two more articulate Highwaymen would be sleeping in the best rooms at the further end of the long corridor which connected with his.

He was not mistaken.

Rigg had been awakened perhaps by the sound of voices downstairs or perhaps by an instinct of danger.

At the first creak of the door opening, Rigg snatched up his pistol.

As it opened wider still, he fired.

His bullet missed the Marquis but grazed the soldier behind him.

The soldier immediately fired back, and Rigg toppled backwards onto the bed.

Mrs. Gibbons screamed and, picking up his fallen pistol, fired indiscriminately at the soldiers entering the room.

A soldier who did not realise he was firing at a woman fired back, and she too fell to the floor.

By this time Bill and the other Highwaymen in the Servants' Hall had joined in the fray.

One soldier was slightly wounded and Bill received a shot in the arm.

A bullet from his pistol grazed the Marquis's left hand, drawing a little blood.

It was only seconds before the soldiers overpowered the two men and disarmed them.

Then, leaving a Captain who was in command to remove Rigg's dead body and cope with Mrs. Gibbons, who was wounded, the Marquis ran upstairs.

He found Nanny and Imilda on the second floor.

They had not dared to come down, and when the Marquis appeared, Nanny gave a cry of relief.

"You're safe, Master Vulcan, you're safe!" she cried, and the tears were running down her cheeks.

It was Imilda who saw the blood on his hand and exclaimed:

"You are wounded! What has happened?"

"Only a scratch," the Marquis said. "The Highwaymen are all captured, although one is dead, and the Housekeeper is wounded."

"I'm not going to say I'm sorry," Nanny said.

She was putting a bowl on the table as she spoke, and a kettle was on the fire.

Imilda helped the Marquis out of his coat as Nanny insisted, and his wound was cleaned and bandaged.

"Is *Apollo* all right?" Imilda asked.

"He took me to the Barracks in record time," the Marquis answered, "and I left him loose in the paddock, where I knew he would be quite safe while there was such a turmoil going on in the house."

Imilda gave a sigh of relief.

"Now your other horses are safe too," she said.

"So are you and Nanny," the Marquis replied.

Nanny had finished bandaging his hand, and he said:

"I must go down and see what is happening, but I wanted first to make quite sure that neither of you was in trouble."

He looked at Imilda as he spoke.

She felt annoyed with herself, because she blushed.

It was impossible not to think of how he had kissed her goodbye before riding off on *Apollo*.

"I will let you know what is happening very soon," the Marquis said.

He went downstairs.

Nanny took the bowl containing the blood-stained water from his wound into the Bathroom.

"It might have been worse," she said, but Imilda had already gone.

She felt she must see what was happening.

She went down to the first floor and stood on the landing above the hall.

The front-door was open.

Outside, she could see the brake had been brought up from where it had been hidden.

The seven Highwaymen with their hands securely tied behind their backs had been put into it, together with Rigg's dead body.

The mounted soldiers had retrieved their horses from where they had left them.

They were waiting until the Marquis had finished

his conversation with their Captain.

He was obviously thanking the officer for what had been a quick and well-planned operation with only one minor casualty apart from his own grazed hand.

The soldier who had been shot in the arm was also in the brake.

His arm was in a sling.

Imilda thought it was a wise decision to get him back to the Barracks rather than try to treat him in the house.

There was no sign of Mrs. Gibbons.

Imilda was to learn later, that the Marquis had told Abbot to take her immediately to the Doctor in the village.

He was to tell him that when he had treated her he must find somewhere for her to be nursed but not at the Hall.

The Marquis finished his conversations.

He shook the Captain by the hand and then, in a voice they could all hear, he said:

"Thank you very much. You have done an excellent job and I shall certainly commend you all for your rapid response when I came to the Barracks and your most efficient action here."

He paused a moment and then went on:

"I shall call on the General later today and report it to him."

"It has been a pleasure to help you, My Lord," the Captain said.

The men cheered.

It was quite obvious that they had definitely enjoyed what had been an unexpected and real battle in the middle of their manoeuvres.

The brake drove off, the soldiers on horseback on either side of it.

As they turned down the drive, the Marquis came into the house.

Imilda did not move or speak, but he looked up and saw her at the top of the stairs.

"I want to talk to you," he said.

She came down.

As she did so, old Hutton, shaking a little, appeared in the hall.

He was obviously afraid that the Marquis might blame him for what had occurred.

The Marquis merely said:

"I am hungry, Hutton. I would like breakfast as soon as it is possible, and Miss Graham will have it with me."

"Very good, My Lord," Hutton said in a tone of relief, and hurried away.

The Marquis walked towards the Study, and when they entered it, he shut the door.

"I suppose you realise," he said, "that I now have a great deal to do to restore the house to what it was like in the past. And first to engage enough servants to run it properly."

"You mean . . . you are . . . going to . . . stay here?" Imilda asked. "I thought . . . you would . . . go back to . . . London."

"As it happens," the Marquis said, "I cannot go back to London, but that is another story. What I am really asking is if you are prepared to help me?"

Imilda drew in her breath.

It passed through her mind that she could not stay and help him unless she was officially engaged as Housekeeper—the post occupied by Mrs. Gibbons.

If she was known to be a Lady, she would have to be chaperoned.

If the Marquis knew who she was, he could not ask her to stay and help him.

She was silent because she did not know what to answer.

After a moment the Marquis said:

"Having organised everything so perfectly from the moment I arrived, you can hardly abandon me now."

"It is ... not ... that," Imilda replied, "and I am ... sure if you ... really intend ... to stay in ... your home, you could ... organise everything ... yourself."

"I should certainly find it rather dull," the Marquis said, "and I thought, if nothing else, you would help me to enlarge the Stables."

Imilda drew in her breath.

How could she refuse an offer so alluring?

Then the Marquis added:

"Of course you may not wish to be with me and to help me as I want you to. Perhaps you have other plans for the future."

Imilda still did not know what to say.

Without thinking what she was doing, she walked across the room to the open window.

She stood looking out at the fountain in the garden.

It was throwing its water high into the sky, and the sun turned every drop into a rainbow.

'Nothing could be so lovely,' Imilda thought.

Then the Marquis was beside her, and as she turned to look up at him enquiringly, he said very softly:

"When I kissed you goodbye early this morning, I thought it was the most exciting thing that had ever happened to me. Now I want to make quite sure I was not mistaken."

Before Imilda could move, before she could understand what he was saying, his arms were around her.

147

His lips took hers captive.

As he touched her, she felt the same streak of lightning run through her body.

At the same time, it seemed as if it were the rainbow from the fountain.

At first his lips were very gentle.

Then, as he felt her quiver, he held her closer still and his kiss became more possessive, more insistent.

Imilda could not move, could not think!

She could only feel the sensation and ecstasy which was different from anything she had ever known, yet it seemed part of everything she had found beautiful and perfect.

The Marquis kissed her for a long time.

Then, as he raised his head, he said in a voice which was deep and unsteady:

"How can either of us fight against that?"

Imilda looked up at him and her eyes were shining.

"What do you feel about me," he asked very quietly.

"I love . . . you . . . of course . . . I love . . . you," Imilda whispered. "But so . . . many women have . . . told you . . . that."

"What I am going to say to you," the Marquis replied, "is something which I swear on the Bible I have never said to any woman."

He paused before he said very quietly:

"I love you, I love you with my heart and my soul. How soon, my Darling, will you marry me?"

Now Imilda started.

She had forgotten for the time being that she had run away and why.

His kiss had taken her up into the sky and she felt as if she were in Heaven.

Now she moved to hide her face against his shoulder.

"I have . . . something to . . . tell . . . you," she said in a voice he could hardly hear.

"What is it?" the Marquis asked.

"I am . . . not who you . . . think I . . . am," Imilda whispered. "I am . . . in . . . hiding."

"In hiding?" the Marquis questioned. "From whom?"

After what seemed a long silence, Imilda whispered:

"From . . . you."

The Marquis drew her a little closer still, then put his fingers under her chin and turned her face up to his.

"Did you really think, my adorable one," he said, "that I did not know who you were?"

Imilda gasped.

"You know that I am Imilda Bourne?"

"When you came to my Bedroom," the Marquis said, "to tell me to get up and hide in the secret passage, you were whispering. But I felt sure I had heard that soft little voice before, telling me what I ought to do."

"You . . . remembered . . . me?" Imilda murmured.

"I did what you told me," the Marquis said. "I went to the House of Lords and made a speech asking for something to be done for the men who were returning from the Army of Occupation."

"You did . . . that, you . . . really did . . . that because I . . . asked . . . you?" Imilda murmured.

"I had my orders," the Marquis said as he smiled, "just as, my adorable one, you have given me orders ever since I came here."

"You have . . . carried them . . . out so . . . brilliantly," Imilda said, "that I was . . . afraid you . . . would . . . not want . . . me any . . . more."

"I want you all the more," the Marquis said, "and I have no intention of losing you. I know now what I want for the future."

"What . . . is . . . that?" Imilda asked a little nervously.

"I want this house, which I have been hating and swearing that I would never come back to again, to be a home. I want a wife who will look after me and love me and will also love my children."

Imilda gave a little sob and hid her face once again on his shoulder.

"I do . . . not believe . . . I am . . . hearing . . . this," she whispered. "I loved . . . this house . . . from the . . . moment I . . . saw it, and then I was . . . upset about the . . . little boy who was . . . so unhappy here. Nanny had told me . . . about him and I kept . . . thinking of . . . him."

"And you wanted to make him happy?" the Marquis said. "That, my Precious one, is exactly what I want you to do."

Imilda looked up at him with tears in her eyes.

"You really . . . think you . . . could be . . . happy here and make the people . . . who work for . . . you happy?"

"You were absolutely right in what you said to me when I was staying at Harsbourne," the Marquis said. "I discovered at the House of Lords that some Landlords have behaved much better than I have."

He stopped for a moment and then continued:

"The Duke of Buccleuch, after my speech, told me that since the end of the war he has taken no rent from his farmers and has refrained from coming to London so that he could afford to pay his retainers."

"That was kind," Imilda cried.

"And Lord Bridgewater informed me he had increased the number he employs on his Estate and in his house from five to eight hundred persons."

"Is that what . . . you intend to . . . do?" Imilda asked.

"That and very much more," the Marquis replied, "as long as you will help me."

"You . . . know that is . . . what I want . . . to do," Imilda whispered. "But . . . suppose that when . . . we are . . . married you become . . . bored with . . . me."

The Marquis laguhed.

"I know that is impossible," he said. "You have surprised, intrigued, and, at the same time, ordered me about ever since I have known you. Now when I kiss you I know that what I feel is totally different from anything I have ever felt before."

He paused for a moment and then, with his eyes twinkling, he said:

"I will explain to you the difference, but I think we should get married first."

"How can . . . we do . . . that?" Imilda asked, "without . . . going back . . . to London."

"It is quite simple," the Marquis replied. "There is a private Chapel here in the house which was locked up on my Stepmother's order. I intend to open it immediately. The Vicar, when I had tea with him, hinted that he would like to be my private Chaplain."

He hesitated, then went on:

"We can get married tonight or tomorrow, if you agree, and then start our work in the house and on the Estate. It will be, if nothing else, a very unusual honeymoon!"

Imilda looked up at him and then she said:

"Are . . . you quite . . . certain you . . . want me and

that you are not . . . making a . . . mistake?"

"I am quite, quite certain," the Marquis answered. "Now I am marrying, not because I was trapped into it, but because I want it more than I have ever wanted anything in my life before."

There was no doubt of the sincerity in his voice.

Then, as his lips were on hers, there was no need for Imilda to answer him.

The following day she and the Marquis rode in the morning.

Then he told her he was going to be very busy arranging their wedding.

It was to take place in the evening, and she was to rest.

"I will do that," she said. "But first I will do a little work in the Herb Garden. As soon as you have arranged everything else, I want two Gardeners to help me. Then I can make sure you are always fit and well, because I shall have the right herbs to give you."

The Marquis pulled her into his arms.

He kissed first her forehead, then her eyes and her straight little nose.

"I love and adore you," he said. "You shall have a hundred Gardeners if you want them. But first we must try and make our home a little more shipshape."

"I heard that you told Hutton to engage six footmen," Imilda said, "and they are all to be men who served in the Army."

"I am taking on a large number of men from every village on my Estate," the Marquis said.

He did not add that he had been tremendously moved by the eagerness with which the men had accepted his offer of work.

Mr. Richardson who, as Imilda had suspected, was not ill, but frightened, was back in his office.

He was vastly increasing the list of wages he must pay out every Friday.

In the Kitchen Mrs. Hutton had burst into tears when she was told she could have four or five women and two scullions to help her.

Nanny was very busy engaging girls from the village to be housemaids.

She said she could manage until they could find an experienced Housekeeper to take Mrs. Gibbons's place.

There was so much going on that the whole house seemed to buzz like a beehive.

When Imilda came in from the Herb Garden to rest on her bed, she knew the whole atmosphere had changed.

She was quite certain that the Marquis's Mother was looking down with approval.

Her son was restoring the happiness there had been at the Hall when she was Chatelaine.

Imilda thought that as soon as she was married she would write to her Father and tell him she was safe and well.

She would not say where she was.

She had no wish for her Stepmother to come to Melverley Hall and spoil the happiness that seemed to grow every hour of the day.

"There is no hurry," she told herself.

Then, as if he knew what she was thinking, the Marquis said:

"Let us wait until we feel strong enough to cope with other people. Then we will put in the Court Circular that our marriage has taken place."

Even as he spoke he wondered if that would be possible.

If the *Conte* died, he would have to go abroad.

Even so, he knew, as he could take Imilda with him, it would not be for him the disaster it would have been.

Every time he was near her he felt he loved her more, and wanted the house to be perfect for her.

He felt the evil atmosphere was being swept away.

The happiness he had known with his Mother was restored and he could feel her presence in the rooms which had been specially hers.

Her Bedroom had been closed on his Father's orders when she died.

Even his Stepmother had not been brave enough to open it.

Now the whole staff had helped to dust and clean it.

The Gardeners had brought in the flowers he had ordered, to decorate the Bedroom and also the Chapel.

Lying upstairs, knowing the Marquis was thinking only of her, Imilda wished she had a really beautiful wedding-gown to wear.

There was only a soft white muslin dress amongst those she had packed for *Apollo* to carry.

She felt it was really too simple.

She had no idea that as it clung to her figure it made her look like the goddess from Olympus which the Marquis had said she might be.

When Nanny said it was time for her to have her bath and dress, she put on the white muslin gown.

Nanny brought from her room a very beautiful Brussels lace veil.

She told Imilda the Marquis's Mother had worn it

when she married. Several other Countesses of Melverley had also worn it before her.

There was an exquisite diamond tiara which Imilda had not expected, a necklace to match it, and diamond earrings.

Imilda put them on and looked at herself in the mirror.

She knew she looked exactly like the bride the Marquis should have.

It was the way she wanted him to think of her on their wedding-day.

One of the new footmen, rather self-conscious in his livery, knocked on the door.

He said His Lordship was waiting, but Nanny was to go down first to be in the Chapel before them.

Imilda was aware that only the old servants whom the Marquis had known as a boy would be present in the Chapel.

Nanny, wearing her very best bonnet, hurried down the stairs.

Imilda waited for a few seconds, then picked up the bouquet which the footman had put down on a table and started down the stairs.

She had the feeling she was stepping into a new and strange world.

But the Marquis would enjoy teaching her about it and she need not be afraid.

"I love ... him ... I love ... him," she told herself.

It did not matter what other people might think of him and his behaviour since the war.

She knew she was a part of him, and they had lived together in another life before they were re-united in this.

He was waiting for her in the hall as she came down the Grand Staircase.

Her heart did several somersaults at the sight of him looking so handsome.

He was wearing his decorations.

Imilda thought that even if their wedding was the most important Social event of the year in London, neither of them could look more glamorous.

She did not know, and she was not to know until long afterwards, that the Marquis had received a wedding-present.

It was more important to him than any other could have been.

It was a letter from Charlie, and it said:

> *"The* Comte *has recovered enough to go back to Italy. He will not die and the Prince Regent intends to ignore the whole episode. Therefore there is no reason for you not to come back to London. Make it soon because I miss you.*
>
> Charles.*"*

The Marquis had no intention anyway of going to London for a long time.

But this meant the menace that had sent him to the country involuntarily was now withdrawn.

"Good comes out of evil," he said to himself. "If I had not had to hide, I would not have found Imilda and realised how much she meant to me."

As she reached the bottom of the stairs, he took her hands in his.

He raised one after the other to his lips.

"I love you," he said, "and you are the most beautiful person I have seen in my whole life."

He meant it, for he knew she had something else that no other woman with whom he had made love had ever had.

It was a spirituality which seemed to shine through her beauty.

It captured not only his heart, but his soul.

They went towards the Chapel.

The Vicar and the older members of the household were waiting and an organ was being played very softly by someone who could not be seen.

The flowers which decorated the altar scented the whole Chapel.

As soon as Imilda entered the Chapel, she knew it was exactly as she wanted the Chapel belonging to Melverley to be.

She and the Marquis with their children would worship there and bring to it all their troubles and difficulties.

Now she had come to it in happiness.

As she looked up at the Marquis and saw the love in his eyes, she knew God had blessed them both.

They had found together the real love which comes from Him.

The Vicar read the Marriage Service with a sincerity which was very moving.

When they knelt for the blessing, Imilda slipped her hand into the Marquis's.

He was feeling as she did that their marriage was something they would never forget or spoil.

Then they went into the Drawing-Room, where the rest of the Household joined them to toast Imilda and the Marquis in Champagne.

Hutton made a little speech, Nanny wept, and it was all very moving.

Then the Bride and Bridegroom went upstairs.

The Marquis took Imilda into a room she had never seen. It had been his Mother's Bedroom.

That too was decorated with flowers, and they were all lilies.

"They are like you, my Precious," the Marquis said softly.

Then they went into the Boudoir next door.

It was beautifully decorated, and waiting for them was a cold dinner to which they could help themselves.

There was Champagne in a golden ice-cooler.

There were flowers everywhere, and as Imilda looked at them, the Marquis put his arms around her.

"You are my wife," he said. "I have won the battle to make you love me. Now you are mine, and no-one, my Precious, shall ever take you from me."

He moved his lips over the softness of her skin and added:

"I shall be a very jealous Husband. If any rascal like the Marquis of Melverley, for instance, comes near you, I shall kill him, and make no mistake, I am a very good shot."

Imilda laughed.

"You forget that I would have a part in that, Darling," she said, "and I know that I could never look at any man except you. If I did, he would not be as handsome as you, as kind as you, or, more important than anything else, as wonderful as you."

The Marquis pulled her closer and she could say no more.

Late that night Imilda stirred against her Husband's shoulder.

"Are you awake, my Precious?" he asked.

"How can I sleep," she answered, "when I am so happy? Oh, why, Vulcan, did no-one ever tell me how wonderful love is?"

The Marquis smiled.

"It is wonderful for us," he said, "because I know that we are part of each other, and I want to say something else to you, my perfect little wife."

Imilda was listening, and he said:

"You know my reputation, you know there have been many women in my life, but I swear I have never until now known, like you, that love was so wonderful."

"You really mean," Imilda asked, "that I . . . am . . . different?"

"Very, very different," he answered.

There was just one candle shining behind the curtain which fell from the corona on top of the bed.

Very gently he ran his finger down her face and said:

"Other women I have known have been beautiful, but your beauty, my Darling, comes from inside you and is part of your soul."

He paused, still looking at her before he continued:

"I not only adore you because you excite me as a man, but I worship you because you are good and pure. You give me a love which I have known only once before, and that was from my Mother."

"Oh, Darling, that is what I want . . . you to . . . think," Imilda said. "When we have . . . children, and I hope . . . we have lots, we will make them feel that this, our home, is the happiest place in the world! It is where they can always come back to and will always be welcome."

The Marquis knew she was thinking of him and the unhappiness he had suffered at the hands of his Stepmother.

"That is a vow," he said "and that is another reason, my Darling, adorable little wife, that I could never in the future look at any woman except you."

"I love . . . you," Imilda said. "Love me . . . please love . . . me."

Then, as the Marquis made her his, she knew that the blessing of God which they had felt in the Chapel was still with them.

It would be theirs all through their lives.

They had found the love which comes from Heaven and goes on into Eternity.

ABOUT THE AUTHOR

Barbara Cartland, the world's most famous romantic novelist, who is also an historian, playwright, lecturer, political speaker and television personality, has now written 621 books and sold over six hundred and fifty million copies all over the world.

She has also had many historical works published and has written four autobiographies as well as the biographies of her mother and that of her brother, Ronald Cartland, who was the first Member of Parliament to be killed in the last war. This book has a preface by Sir Winston Churchill and has been republished with an introduction by Sir Arthur Bryant.

Love at the Helm, a novel written with the help and inspiration of the late Earl Mountbatten of Burma, Great Uncle of His Royal Highness, The Prince of Wales, is being sold for the Mountbatten Memorial Trust.

She has broken the world record for the last twenty-one years by writing an average of twenty-three books a year. In the *Guinness Book of World Records* she is listed as the world's top-selling author.

Miss Cartland in 1987 sang an Album of Love Songs with the Royal Philharmonic Orchestra.

In private life Barbara Cartland, who is a Dame of the Order of St. John of Jerusalem and Chairman of the St. John Council in Hertfordshire, has fought for better conditions and salaries for Midwives and Nurses.

She championed the cause for the Elderly in 1956, invoking a Government Enquiry into the "Housing Condition of Old People."

In 1962 she had the Law of England changed so that Local Authorities had to provide camps for their own Gypsies. This has meant that since then thousands and thousands of Gypsy children have been able to go to School, which they had never been able to do in the past, as their caravans were moved every twenty-four hours by the Police.

There are now fifteen camps in Hertfordshire and Barbara Cartland has her own Romany Gypsy Camp called "Barbaraville" by the Gypsies.

Her designs "Decorating with Love" are being sold all over the U.S.A. and the National Home Fashions League made her, in 1981, "Woman of Achievement."

She is unique in that she was one and two in the Dalton list of Best Sellers, and one week had four books in the top twenty.

Barbara Cartland's book *Getting Older, Growing Younger* has been published in Great Britain and the U.S.A. and her fifth cookery book, *The Romance of Food*, is now being used by the House of Commons.

In 1984 she received at Kennedy Airport America's Bishop Wright Air Industry Award for her contribution to the development of aviation. In 1931 she and two R.A.F. Officers thought of, and carried, the first aeroplane-towed glider airmail.

During the War she was Chief Lady Welfare Officer in Bedfordshire, looking after 20,000 Servicemen and women. She thought of having a pool of Wedding Dresses at the War Office so a Service Bride could hire a gown for the day.

She bought 1,000 gowns without coupons for the A.T.S., the W.A.A.F.'s and the W.R.E.N.S. In 1945 Barbara Cartland received the Certificate of Merit from Eastern Command.

In 1964 Barbara Cartland founded the National Association for Health of which she is the President, as a front for all the Health Stores and for any product made as alternative medicine.

This is now a £65 million turnover a year, with one-third going in export.

In January 1968 she received *La Médeille de Vermeil de la Ville de Paris*. This is the highest award to be given in France by the City of Paris. She has sold 30 million books in France.

In March 1988 Barbara Cartland was asked by the Indian Government to open their Health Resort outside Delhi. This is almost the largest Health Resort in the world.

Barbara Cartland was received with great enthusiasm by her fans, who feted her at a reception in the City, and she received the gift of an embossed plate from the Government.

Barbara Cartland was made a Dame of the Order of the British Empire in the 1991 New Year's Honours List by Her Majesty, The Queen, for her contribution to Literature and also for her years of work for the community.

Dame Barbara has now written 621 books, the greatest number by a British author, passing the 564 books written by John Creasey.

1945   Received Certificate of Merit, Eastern Command, for being Welfare Officer to 5,000 troops in Bedfordshire.

1953   Made a Commander of the Order of St. John of Jerusalem. Invested by H.R.H. The Duke of Gloucester at Buckingham Palace.

1972   Invested as Dame of Grace of the Order of St. John in London by The Lord Prior, Lord Cacia.

1981   Received "Achiever of the Year" from the National Home Furnishing Association in Colorado Springs, U.S.A., for her designs for wallpaper and fabrics.

1984   Received Bishop Wright Air Industry Award at Kennedy Airport, for inventing the aeroplane-towed Glider.

1988   Received from Monsieur Chirac, The Prime Minister, The Gold Medal of the City of Paris, at the Hotel de la Ville, Paris, for selling 25 million books and giving a lot of employment.

1991   Invested as Dame of the Order of The British Empire, by H.M. The Queen at Buckingham Palace for her contribution to Literature.